The Curious Cape Cod Skull

The Curious Cape Cod Skull

Marie Lee

Marie Lee

AVALON BOOKS
THOMAS BOUREGY AND COMPANY, INC.
401 LAFAYETTE STREET
NEW YORK, NEW YORK 10003

© Copyright 1995 by Marie Lee
Library of Congress Catalog Card Number 94-96731
ISBN 0-8034-9109-3

PRINTED IN THE UNITED STATES OF AMERICA
ON ACID-FREE PAPER
BY HADDON CRAFTSMEN, SCRANTON, PENNSYLVANIA

To John,
for your patience and support,
and especially for sacrificing your morning
walks

Author's Note

Eastham is a picturesque town slightly above the elbow of Cape Cod. It is inhabited by wonderful and interesting people, none of whom appear in this book, which is a work of fiction.

In November, 1990, a storm caused severe erosion at Coast Guard Beach, and the National Park Service decided to excavate the site, resulting in the discovery of artifacts estimated to be ten thousand years old. The archaeological dig in this book is fictional and occurs three years later, after another storm.

Acknowledgment is made of the assistance extended to the author by Donald A. Watson, police chief of Eastham. Police procedure described correctly is due to his generous explanations. Errors in police procedure are the author's own.

Newcomb Family Tree

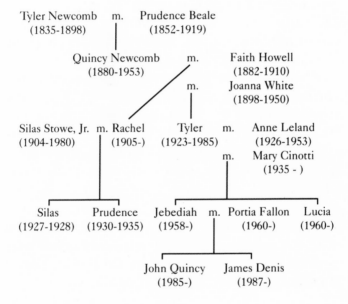

Tyler Newcomb   m.   Prudence Beale
(1835-1898)   (1852-1919)

Quincy Newcomb   m.   Faith Howell
(1880-1953)   (1882-1910)
                                    m.   Joanna White
                                            (1898-1950)

Silas Stowe, Jr. m. Rachel   Tyler   m.   Anne Leland
(1904-1980)   (1905-)   (1923-1985)   (1926-1953)
                                          m.   Mary Cinotti
                                                  (1935 -)

Silas   Prudence   Jebediah m. Portia Fallon   Lucia
(1927-1928) (1930-1935) (1958-)   (1960-)   (1960-)

John Quincy   James Denis
(1985-)   (1987-)

"Death is a debt to nature due:
As I have paid it so must you."

Inscription on the gravestone
of Deacon Samuel Doane
Bridge Road Cemetery
Eastham, Massachusetts

Chapter One

The body might not have been discovered for months if Marguerite had not gone down to the shed for the clam pail and rakes, relegated to storage status after her children had acquired more interest in fellow mammals than in mollusks. Secretly, she had been relieved to abandon clam digging with its resultant cut fingers and muck-covered legs and arms redolent of the bivalves whose domiciles she invaded. Clam chowder was easily purchased ready-to-eat or as chowder base, both purportedly home-made (whose home? she wondered). But today her nephew Jeb and his two sons, aged six and eight, were arriving. Sunday morning clamming at Salt Pond was high on Marguerite's list of experiences for children. Never mind that few children actually liked eating clams.

The first surprise of her day was finding the shed locked. The padlock hanging on the hasp was only used to keep the door closed; she never snapped it. Until recently, there had never been a lock on the door, but the recurring reports of coyotes in Eastham had impelled Marguerite to keep the door firmly shut. Mice, voles, chipmunks, and other diminutive animals still entered through the chinks in the old boards and nested in the relics of the past, never to be used but never to be discarded. Marguerite tried to live in harmony with nature, but that did not include housing a coyote den, particularly since her dog, Rusty, was a city dog and more likely to be wary of cars than of coyote parents with hungry pups.

"Rusty, I was afraid my mind would deteriorate when I retired, but it has only been two months. I can't believe I snapped that lock," she said aloud, shaking her head and causing her dark, curly hair to bounce playfully about her head. Talking to the dog was, to Marguerite's mind, less suspect than talking to one's self.

Rusty seemed disturbed at the delay, as she was barking furiously and scratching at the door, uncharacteristic behavior for a dog who always demurred at entering that dark haven of discarded treasures. Back to the cellar trudged Marguerite, hoping she would find the key and beginning to perspire from the heat of this July Saturday, excessive by Cape Cod standards. The key was soon found, its holder back down to the old well shed—long bereft of a well—and the key inserted into the lock.

"Move back, girl, or I'll never get this door open."

The usual musty smell of the shed was worse than ever and particularly offensive.

"I should get a screen door so that I could air this place in the summer," she mused.

In the darkness, the body first appeared to be a man sleeping. Only upon approaching did Marguerite see the blood covering the face and the unnaturalness of the position, arms above the head, stretched straight out, palms supine, fingers clenched. The legs were also straight out and slightly parted. The dog was alternately barking and whining as she circled the body.

With her gorge rising, Marguerite rushed out of the shed, grabbing the dog's collar as she went. Leaning against a tree, she recovered her equanimity and reswallowed her breakfast to the cacophony of continued barking.

"Suppose he is not dead but only unconscious. I have to go back in there. He might need help."

Slipping through the door and closing it after her so as not to admit the dog, Marguerite found it difficult to see. Groping along the perimeter of the body, she located the wrist and put her fingers on the pressure point. No pulse. Braver now that the increased darkness concealed the blood, she felt for the temple. No pulse.

Marguerite left the shed again and noted some congealed blood on her fingers. Reluctant to wipe them on her shorts, she picked up a piece of paper lying near the door, wiped her fingers, put the paper in her shorts for later disposal, and considered her next moves. First, lock the shed; second, call the police; third, call Jeb and prevent him from coming with the boys; fourth, vomit at leisure. Science teachers, even retired ones, think in outline form.

"Rusty, let's go. We have a lot to do and I suppose the police will want me to keep you out of this area. You may have to remain inside, so don't start complaining."

The telephone had a neat orange sticker with a phone number to report an emergency or fire.

"I guess this qualifies as an emergency." Marguerite dialed, then, "I want to report a dead body."

The phone was answered on the second ring.

"Stowe residence, Ms. Silva speaking."

"Ms. Silva, this is Marguerite Smith. Is my nephew, Jeb, there?"

"No, he left a few minutes ago. I believe he was on his way to your house."

"Oh, no! I was hoping to stop him."

"Is anything wrong?"

"Er . . . no. Er . . . no need to worry, Aunt Rachel. I just had a change of plans. 'Bye, now."

* * *

There were no sirens or flashing blue lights. Just one patrol car pulled into the driveway and a young policeman reluctantly walked toward the deck.

To police officers on Cape Cod, the graying of America was more evident than it was to their brother officers in other locales. All too often the police handled calls from a panicked retiree whose spouse had expired. Far from family, miles from their physicians, the police were their only recourse. Calming the distressed bereaved was the first order of business and the most difficult.

Too nervous to await him, Marguerite ran out to meet him. "Officer, something terrible has happened!"

"Yes, I know. Why don't we go inside and talk about it?"

"Not in the house! In the shed!"

"What's in the shed?"

"The body!"

"Was he working in the shed?"

"No. I don't know how he got there."

"We had better go and look."

"This way. The door is locked, but I have the key."

Officer David Morgan, two years a policeman, all of it in Eastham, had never seen a murder victim. He had helped remove a dead accident victim from her car, had seen bodies of people who died at home of natural causes, and had even assisted in recovering a drowning victim who had fallen through the ice on a pond, but murder! The blood! The smell! The body lying as if stretched on a rack! Evil permeated the little shed. He visibly shrank in on himself. Now it was Marguerite who offered support.

"Come out here and get some air. It's hard to breathe in there."

"Yes. Yes, I will. But I have to make sure he's dead," in a weak voice.

Poorly hiding his repugnance, Officer Morgan bent down and made an attempt to find a pulse. Assisted by light from his flashlight, he quickly came to the same conclusion as Marguerite. Stumbling outside, he attempted to recover his demeanor.

"Who is that?"

"I don't know. It was dark and his face was covered with blood so I am not certain, but I don't think I know him. I certainly don't know how he got in my shed."

"Put the lock on again and give me the key. I have to radio headquarters."

"Aunt Meg! Aunt Meg! Why is that police car here?" Johnny, John Quincy Newcomb, aged eight, was at once struggling with his seat belt, opening the door, and calling out excitedly. Jamie, James Denis Newcomb, aged six, resignedly said nothing. Once again too late to preempt his older, more aggressive brother, he sat quietly, chafing at his perceived inadequacy.

Leisurely, with fluidity of motion, their father, Jeb, emerged from the car. Jebediah Newcomb, the tall, dark, handsome stranger promised by generations of gypsy fortune-tellers to wistful young maidens, was Marguerite's nephew-in-law, married to her niece, Portia.

"Hi, Aunt Margie. Breaking the speed laws again?"

Marguerite cringed. Of all the diminutives for Marguerite, Marge and Margie were the ones she detested. No point in reminding Jeb of this again. It would have no effect other than to label her as churlish.

"It's serious, Jeb. I called Aunt Rachel's house to stop you from coming, but you had already left. Let's get into the house." Marguerite was bursting with the news but anxious to shield the boys.

"Aunt Meg, are you being arrested?" Jamie chirped, inserting a comment into Johnny's parroting of ''What happened? What happened? What happened?''

''Inside, boys,'' said Jeb, suddenly serious.

Marguerite closed the glass door despite the heat as two additional official vehicles turned into the street and squeezed into her driveway.

''For God's sake, Aunt Marge! What's going on?''

''There's a dead body in my shed.''

''No! There can't be. He can't be dead!''

Chapter Two

Francis "Frank" Nadeau, police chief of Eastham, strode purposefully from the shed toward the house, removing his hat and wiping the perspiration from his brow as he walked. His white uniform shirt clung to his wet torso. The sun was high overhead, promising a perfect beach day.

Frank was one of a special genre, a native Cape Codder. His ancestors had settled in Eastham more than two hundred years ago, part of the southward migration of Acadians deported from Nova Scotia by the British because of the imminence of war with France and the question of Acadian neutrality. Immortalized by the poem "Evangeline," the majority of the Acadians settled in Louisiana, enriching that state with their French culture and cuisine.

As a young man, Frank had felt stifled by the insularity of the Cape, surrounded on three sides by ocean, cut adrift from the mainland by the Cape Cod Canal. He joined the Army to see the world. What he saw was Vietnam. Still a small war, not yet pricking the national consciousness, it nevertheless seared his soul and made him long for the clear sky and clean sand of Cape Cod and, mostly, for its ordered and orderly lifestyle.

Enlistment over, he returned home, joined the police force, and never regretted either his leaving or his returning.

7

"Marguerite, who is that in your well shed?"

"Chief, do you think we could delay this for a few minutes? My nephew, Jeb, was just leaving with his boys." Marguerite was attempting to shepherd two bug-eyed boys and their catatonic father toward the door as she spoke. Rusty barked furiously at the chief, the boys resisted moving so much as an inch, and Jeb stared fixedly in the direction of the shed.

"No one is going anywhere," declared the chief curtly. "This is the scene of a crime and everyone will be questioned. The shed, the woods, and the walk are out-of-bounds to everyone including the dog, especially the dog—and the kids."

Turning his attention to Officer Morgan, who was standing listlessly on the path, uncertain of his role now that the medical examiner had arrived and the crime prevention and control (CPAC) unit was awaited, the chief bellowed, "Morgan, get up here and make yourself useful. Take notes."

The latter instruction was more from necessity than from imperiousness. The chief did not routinely answer police calls. Only the distressed message from Officer Morgan announcing an apparent murder brought him to the scene minus the familiar police appurtenance, a notebook.

"Chief, *les garçons*," indicating the two boys. Marguerite unhesitantly spoke in French to Chief Nadeau. She had first met him in the library, where she had heard him asking for books written in French. Fluent in that language through her French-Canadian mother, Marguerite offered to lend him some of her French books when the librarian replied in the negative.

Although many generations removed from his French-speaking ancestors, Frank had a passion for the history of the Acadians that led him to study French diligently in high school and at the community college. To the chagrin of his wife, who longed for tropical beaches, they spent most of their vacations in Canada, where Frank delighted in displaying his conversational ability. Pleased to discover in Eastham someone who shared his cultural roots, he borrowed Marguerite's books and fastened paper clips to the pages with which he had difficulty. Marguerite graciously assisted him, one paper clip at a time.

"*Oui, Marguerite. Peut-être les envoyez au terrain de jeu,*" suggested the chief.

The school playground was just across the road from the house. Grasping Johnny and Jamie firmly by their hands, she marched the boys, clad only in neon-colored bathing suits (chosen by Portia for their visibility, disliked by Jeb for their commonness), through the driveway crammed with official vehicles and across the road to the playground. This was usually the first destination of the boys when they visited, but today it held no attraction.

"Aunt Meg, we want to see the body."

"Is there blood all over?"

"Did you see the murderer?"

Absurd to think that one can shield children when murder and mayhem are only a flick of the television dial away.

Marguerite persisted. "Play here just a little while. I'll call you when your dad is ready to take you to the beach. I have a new yellow tube you can use. And you can practice for the sand castle contest."

Johnny capitulated rather more quickly than usual. Jamie necessarily concurred.

When Marguerite returned to her house, Chief Nadeau had established Jeb's name, address, occupation, and relationship to Marguerite. Jeb was seated at the kitchen table nervously scratching first one leg then the other.

"How long have you been here?" the chief continued.

"I drove up with my sons just a few minutes before you arrived."

"Were you here at any time last night?"

"No, I was not."

"That's all for now, but we may have more questions later."

Before the chief could turn his attention to Marguerite, he was distracted by the arrival of two vehicles, both maneuvering into a neighbor's driveway across the narrow side road. One, a van, carried the CPAC team, who immediately began to assemble photographic equipment and an assortment of satchels barely restraining a plethora of plastic envelopes, rubber gloves, tweezers, magnifiers, powders, brushes, and all the canny paraphernalia calculated to uncover the secrets of a crime scene.

From the second vehicle emerged a state police detective assigned to the district attorney of Barnstable County. He would take charge of the crime scene and coinvestigate the murder with the Eastham police.

Frank exited the house and advanced toward the new arrivals. Detective Albert Medeiros, chunkily filling his uniform, greeted the chief teasingly. "Well, Frank, you finally figured out a way to get me here to do your work for you."

"It's about time someone put you to work," Frank retorted, patting the detective's expanding waistline.

"Good Portuguese cooking, Frank. Nothing like it."

"How did you guys get here so fast? You must have been sitting at the rotary waiting for my call."

"You're damn near right about that. We were in Brewster doing one of our public relations show-and-tell things at the summer fair when the call came. We were glad to have an excuse to hurry out of there. Crime is a cinch compared with standing in the sun answering a thousand questions—actually the same one or two questions hundreds of times—and guarding the equipment from being messed up by grubby little cotton-candied hands. Thanks for the rescue.''

''When we catch the murderer you can thank him personally. I just work here.''

Greetings over, Frank led Detective Medeiros and the two impatient scene of the crime experts across the road to the driveway and down the now well-trodden path to the shed.

Dr. Ernest Wilson was sitting on an upturned cement block and fanning himself with a large index card from his medical bag. Having completed a cursory examination of the victim and confirmed that he was indeed dead, apparently from foul play, he could do no more in the dark shed until lights were set up and the initial photographs taken, allowing him to examine the body more closely and turn it over for posterior inspection.

''I hope you're not sitting on the evidence, Doc,'' said Medeiros, pointing to the cement block.

''If I didn't sit on something I would fall down dead of impatience waiting for you guys. I can't do anything more until you light it up,'' grumpily explained the doctor.

''I'm glad to see you dressed formally for the occasion,'' continued Medeiros.

The doctor was garbed in yellow pants, sneakers, and a hot pink T-shirt advertising Key West.

''You're lucky I'm here at all. I was on my way out of the door when the phone rang, on my way to Hyannis Airport to meet my daughter, her husband, and my three-month-old granddaughter whom I have never seen. They live in England and are visiting for three weeks. I didn't answer the phone, but Pat thought it might be our daughter calling and answered it. Is she sorry! She's on her way to the airport now in the traffic, and the lobsters she was supposed to pick up got a reprieve and are still swimming

around at Captain Jonah's. Guess that will be my job now.''
Doc sighed.

This playful banter of doctor and detective did not reflect
a lack of seriousness at a crime scene. Rather, it was the
professional's way of coping with the distasteful and depressing aspects of murder. It was a manifestation of adults
bonding in their mutual but unspoken disgust with deprav-
ity.

Undeterred by the apparent inertia of their colleagues,
the forensic team was busy organizing the apparatus. Lights
were set up on a collapsible tripod, an extension wire run
up to the house, pictures taken of the entire area, inside and
outside the shed and its environs.

"You can come in now, Doctor," announced Robert
Maleski, the senior of the team. "We have the pictures and
marked the position. If you need more light we can move
this one closer or get another tripod from the van."

"This will do nicely," the doctor responded and entered
the shed. He reexamined the battered, blood-covered head,
noted again the body position, and looked closely at the
upstretched hands and fingers. He then turned over the body
and felt carefully the back of the head and neck. The tou-
sled blond hair was free of blood in the back, but was
fouled by dirt and bits of leaves and pine needles. The
doctor scanned the area around the body, but found no
leaves or needles or compacted dirt, only the expected ac-
cumulations of dust.

"That's interesting," murmured the doctor.

"What's interesting?" called Chief Nadeau through the
opened door.

"The back of the head. The hair has leaves and dirt
caught in it and there are none of those in here. Yet by the
pattern of the blood spattered around the head, it looks as
if he was murdered right here. And while lying down too.''

"You mean he was lying somewhere else, then came here and was killed?" asked Medeiros.

"Could be. Or he may not have come here voluntarily. There's a lump on the back of his head. Probably not enough to kill him, but it could have knocked him out," speculated the doctor.

"That explains the outstretched arms. He was pulled into here unconscious and then killed. But where was he carried from?" pondered the chief.

"That's what you guys get paid for," quipped the doctor. "You might compare the dirt on his head with the dirt outside, but even that won't help you much. He could have gotten that on his head while being dragged. Well, I must be going. You will have my full report first thing in the morning as usual. No, second thing. Pat will insist we go to church to set a good example for the young people. Course I don't know what good that does. They keep telling us that God is in nature, not in a building. Laugh at us for being so old-fashioned. Tell us to sit on the beach at sunrise holding hands and commune with the spirit."

"You can't go yet, Doc. We need more information," protested the chief.

After crawling around that shed, the doctor was dirty and sweaty and smelly. He would need to shower, change his now loathsome clothes, and retrieve those lobsters from their happy abode, all before the family returned. Even that was not guaranteed to spare him from Pat's martyred I-should-have-known-better-than-to-marry-a-doctor look. *I ought to retire, for good this time,* he thought.

"Male Caucasian, and he's dead."

"I know that," sputtered Frank. "How about cause and time?"

Frank, you know I don't do the fancy work. You'll get that from the pathologist after the autopsy."

"Doc, don't pull that little old country doctor routine

with me. This is a murder! We can't investigate without knowing more. Give us your best guess.''

The chief was not overestimating Dr. Wilson's ability to do this. Ernest Wilson had practiced medicine for many years in Philadelphia, where his father and brother had been police officers, captain and lieutenant respectively. Ernest eschewed a career in law enforcement, to the relief of his perpetually worried mother, but seemed to be genetically drawn to it and was a skilled observer of what was meant to be unobservable. As a young doctor he was frequently called to the scene of a crime by his older brother, Henry, then a homicide detective. Ernest soon found himself assisting at and eventually performing autopsies when forensic science was less sophisticated and relied as much on art as on science. Technology intruded on this fellowship of artists. Scene of the crime expertise became a police department speciality; microscopes and gas chronometers given places of honor; DNA uttered in reverence; and over it all ruled the czar of forensics, the state medical examiner, an expert pathologist.

Crime and corpses were never more than intellectual exercises for Ernest, so, as he was gradually eased out of the technostructure of forensic science, his feelings were subtly ambivalent. He was relieved to return to his vocation of healing, but missed the excitement of the chase. His brother continued to discuss cases with him and sometimes asked for his insight on an autopsy report. When the doc moved to Wellfleet, he inevitably became an assistant medical examiner. It was his karma.

"Chief, I don't preempt the pathologist.''

"Just an estimate, Doc. Off the record.''

Reluctantly, Dr. Wilson responded. "Death appears to have been caused by massive head trauma inflicted by a blunt instrument, probably from that baseball bat lying in the poison ivy over there. Of course, the blood will have to be matched by the lab. Time of death was at least ten hours before I examined him, judging from the advanced state of rigor mortis.''

''Can't you narrow that down a bit?'' questioned the chief.

What had started as a small stream of perspiration on the chief was threatening to become a river. The merciless sun taunted him, easily penetrating the grudging bit of shade offered by the pitch pines. Not for the first time did he wish that police departments would adopt the sensible summer dress of the tropics, knee-length shorts and sun helmets. But even the American South resisted this innovation; New England was aeons away from it.

''I'm going to give you a wide range—from eight P.M. to one A.M. Because of the heat, my feeling is later than eight, but anything definite must await the autopsy.''

''Thanks, Doc. That's a lot of time to account for, but at least we don't have to ask where anyone was last week,'' remarked the chief.

''Never grateful, you policemen. Want miracles from us,'' muttered Dr. Wilson. ''Get that stretcher down here,'' he called to the driver of the white van that had just pulled in.

''One moment, Doc,'' called out Detective Medeiros, who had been contemplatively gazing at the crime scene, content to let the chief continue the questioning. ''That cement block you were sitting on—was it in that upright position when you got here?''

''Yes, it was. And it can't be the object on which the deceased hit his head, because it is very wobbly and would have fallen over on impact. I didn't sit on your evidence, Al.''

Medeiros smiled at the perspicaciousness of the doctor. ''I didn't for a minute think you had,'' he replied good-naturedly. ''Go get those lobsters.''

* * *

"Jeb, now that the chief is finished questioning you, why don't you take the boys home?" suggested Marguerite.

"I can't leave you here alone, Aunt Marge, with a murderer in your backyard. We're staying."

Marguerite had not thought of it that graphically, but she was admittedly a little unsettled and was relieved at his emphatic stance.

"Thank you, Jeb, but whatever your decision, you had better take those boys to lunch. There is no way I can feed them now, and I don't know when things will quiet down. Why don't you pick up some sandwiches and take them to the beach until this grisly business is over?"

"I'll take them to lunch, but not to the beach. I'm not feeling well; must have caught a bug. Besides, I won't be able to get out of the driveway with all those police cars. We can walk over to the Clam Shack."

"You certainly seem to have caught something on your legs. You're scratching them to pieces," Marguerite noted.

"It's just some mosquito bites."

"Let me look." Experienced from years of bitten and stung children, Marguerite examined the areas subjected to Jeb's vigorous scratching. "That looks more like a rash than mosquito bites. It looks just like poison ivy. I didn't know you had poison ivy on Beacon Hill. Where have you been walking?"

"Nowhere. It can't be poison ivy. Unless I got it at Aunt Rachel's last evening when I took the boys for a walk on the beach."

"Jeb, there is no poison ivy on the beach."

Chapter Three

Jeb did not have far to look for the boys. As he left the house he spotted the neon bathing suits amidst the verdancy of a copse of trees separating the house from the road and noted two pairs of eyes absorbedly focused on the ghoulish trappings of a murder scene. Little wonder that Johnny had not objected to Marguerite's sidelining him to the playground. He had his own agenda and was rewarded with a ringside location for a grisly sight.

Emerging from the woods, a solemn procession appeared, with Dr. Wilson and his medical bag in the lead followed by a stretcher bearing the bagged body of the murdered man. The upstretched arms, frozen in a position of surrender, did not permit the bag to close fully, necessitating the use of a blanket to cover them. The wheeled stretcher could not negotiate the rough path or the steps and had to be carried, to the dismay of Officer Morgan, who was called to assist the driver. Finally stowed in the van of the medical examiner's office, the body was on its way to the morgue at Barnstable County Hospital in Pocasset.

The narrow road, previously blocked by the van that found no place in Marguerite's or the neighbor's driveways, was now free of impasse, and the small crowd of onlookers who had left their blocked cars and displayed the adamant curiosity common at a police scene found no ex-

17

cuse to linger. A few pedestrians remained, along with two boys and a girl on bicycles who had found kindred souls in Johnny and Jamie and were now crouched beside them behind the bushes, having become the recipients of gratuitous information, everything the Newcomb boys knew or thought they knew. Jeb's appearance interrupted this camaraderie and cleared the copse, much to the relief of the squirrels, intent on finishing their lunch.

Chief Nadeau returned once more from the shed, this time accompanied by Detective Medeiros. Ducking under the yellow tape now stretched around the perimeter of the wooded area, they walked up to the house and entered Marguerite's kitchen. Observing their approach, Marguerite filled four tall glasses with ice, poured into them her rich but clear tea steeped in the rays of the July sun, set a piece of lemon on the edge of each glass, and offered cold drinks to the three officers. Officer Morgan had returned to the kitchen from his service as stretcher-bearer and had turned quite red from the exertion, the heat, and his anxiety at being the recorder for questioning in a murder. He gulped the iced tea in one continuous swallow and sheepishly put the glass on the table. Without comment, Marguerite refilled it and added a fresh piece of lemon. The chief, the detective, and Marguerite, just as thirsty but more inhibited, sipped at their drinks. The chief broke the silence.

He began formally. "Mrs. Smith, Detective Albert Medeiros of the state police. He is assigned to the district attorney's office and is in charge of this case. We shall be working closely with him, so anything you remember after we leave can be communicated to either of us. Right now we would like to ask you some questions to determine if you can help us.

"The victim was Peter Dafoe, with a Cambridge address. He has a membership card to an archaeological society and a faculty library card for King's University. Did you know him?''

''No. I didn't know him or anything about him. There's an archaeological dig out at the beach, though. He might be associated with that.''

''That's what I'm thinking. But how did he end up in such an out-of-the-way place as your shed back in the woods? It's a real stumper. By the way, do you own a baseball bat?''

''Yes, I do. Or at least my son, Neil, does.''

''Where is it now? Is it in the house?''

''No, I put it down in the shed along with a lot of my children's other things that they won't take with them but won't hear of my discarding—like sleds, bicycles, and some odds and ends.''

''Is this bat by chance a Mickey Mantle bat?''

''Let me think. Yes, I believe it is. Joe, that's my ex-husband, looked in several sport stores to get that exact bat. Mantle was Neil's hero that year. But why are you so concerned about Neil's old baseball bat?''

''Because it is now lying in the woods covered with blood. We believe it was the murder weapon.''

Marguerite's enforced calm momentarily deserted her and she shivered despite the heat. The thought of that innocent plaything being used for so foul a purpose was monstrous. She never wanted to see it again, even if the police did offer to return it to her.

In a softer tone, with deference to her shock, the chief addressed her, ''We can only get to the bottom of this if we start at the top. Who was here last night, besides you, at any time after eight P.M.?''

''No one. I was here alone until shortly before eight P.M., when I left to play bridge.''

''No deliveries? No visitors? No dog walkers? No cars going down the lane?''

"I didn't have any deliveries or visitors, but you surely do not expect me to notice anyone walking or driving past. This is July. People go past all the time." Marguerite's voice was slightly scolding.

"I am referring to people acting suspiciously, like walking around repeatedly or cars circling or slowing."

"No, nothing like that," said Marguerite, shaking her head.

"Let's get back to the bridge game. Where did you play?"

"At Laura Eldredge's house."

"Who else was there?"

"Frank, are you asking me for an alibi?" The scolding tone was pronounced now.

"Only going by the book, Marguerite. Nothing personal. After all, the murder was committed on your property, the murder weapon was yours, and you found the body," recited the chief.

Frank did not for a moment think that Marguerite was the murderer. Middle-aged ladies occasionally commit murder, but they prefer a gun or poison. This was a very physical crime involving a lot of battering and the moving of an unconscious man weighing about one hundred and seventy pounds. But he felt that Marguerite held the key. She might not even be aware of it, but there was some reason why the body was in her shed rather than on the anonymous dunes, marshes, or woods abundant in Eastham. He hoped to jog her memory.

"George Atkinson was there and Beatrice Owens," huffily now.

"What time did you leave?"

"I left shortly before ten P.M. We usually play until about ten-thirty, but George's ulcers were acting up again and he left about nine-fifteen or nine-thirty. So Laura served her usual coconut cake and we left early."

"When did you arrive home?"

"At about ten o'clock or a little after. It only takes five or ten minutes from Laura's house."

"Did you notice anything unusual? Anything at all? Sounds, lights, anything disturbed?"

"Now that you mention it, yes. As soon as I came home I let Rusty out. She doesn't like to be out alone in the dark and usually returns to the door in a short while. But last night she stayed out a little longer than usual and then I heard her barking. I went outside and called to her and was surprised to discover she was down by the shed. She rarely goes there—I discourage her because of the ticks—and she never goes there at night. I called her several times, but she continued to bark. Then suddenly she was quiet. I went in the house to get my torch and shone it down the path toward the shed. I just caught Rusty as she ran off into the woods, and then I couldn't see her anymore. This was very strange behavior and I was puzzled but not anxious to explore the woods at night. I continued to call her, and in a few minutes she came running back. I took her inside and concluded she was chasing a rabbit. She cannot resist them. But I did not see or hear anything else."

"What time do you estimate you let the dog out?"

"Shortly after ten o'clock, five or ten minutes. She barks to go out the instant I come home, so I always let her out immediately."

"I think Rusty saw the murderer or the victim. But why did she stop barking? And why did she run off through the woods? Was she following someone? No, she probably would have continued barking. Maybe she was following someone's trail." The chief was ruminating, staring at the ceiling and not expecting an answer. "If only dogs could talk." He sighed.

"They can, Frank. We just don't know how to listen to them," Marguerite offered.

Detective Medeiros interrupted the chief for the first time. "Mrs. Smith, when the dog came back, was she carrying anything in her mouth, even the smallest bit of something?"

"No, she couldn't have been, because she came running up to me with her mouth open as it usually is when she runs."

"Was she cut? Did she have any blood or dirt or anything else on her?" he continued.

"No, she was fine. Nothing at all on her."

"When we are finished here I want you to go to the top of the steps as far as the police tape and direct the forensic team to the area in which you saw the dog run. Do you think you can do that?" Medeiros asked.

"I can show you the approximate direction, but it was dark and I didn't realize it was of any importance."

"That's good enough. Don't go down there yourself, and keep the dog away from the taped area. It is off-limits until further notice. Excuse me for interrupting, Chief. Please continue."

Returning to the sequence of events, the chief queried, "Let's continue with what you did next. I assume you brought the dog into the house. What time?"

"It must have been about ten-thirty or close to it. I didn't look at the clock."

"Then what did you do?"

"I locked up, turned out the downstairs lights, and went upstairs to my room to read," recalled Marguerite.

"Did the dog bark again? Did you see or hear anything else?"

"No. But I wouldn't have been able to hear anything. It was hot upstairs, so I turned on the air conditioner and that drowns out other sounds. After the eleven o'clock news on the radio, I felt too tired to read any longer and went to bed. Of course, I couldn't fall asleep right away. That coconut cake of Laura's is like lead.'' Marguerite and Laura continually sparred over culinary prowess.

"What time did you wake up this morning?"

"Shortly before eight A.M."

"Tell me what you did all morning."

"First, I took Rusty out for a walk. I try to do this at least once a day, because otherwise she just lies around and gets no exercise. Especially now that she is getting a little older. And the walk is good for me too," explained Marguerite. "Then—"

"Wait!" interrupted the chief. "When you let her out, did she run down to the shed or to the woods?"

"No, but I had her on a leash so she couldn't have. I always use a leash when I walk her on the road. One sight of a rabbit and she would dash off in front of a car."

"Okay. Continue."

"We walked for about half or three-quarters of an hour, then we returned and had breakfast. I always give her a little treat in the morning."

"She looks it," declared the chief, eyeing the overweight dog.

"She only got heavy when she got older. Like all of us," retorted Marguerite with a significant glance at the chief's waistline.

"Go on. What did you do next?"

"I cleaned up the breakfast things, made my bed, showered, dressed, and then prepared some chicken salad for Jeb and the boys. I was expecting them around noon. They were supposed to come Friday night, but Jeb called to say he would be here Saturday instead. By the time I finished it was nearly eleven and I decided to go down to the shed and get the clam pail and rakes. We are going clamming in Salt Pond Sunday morning, and I wanted to get the equipment out of the shed before the boys came. I don't like them to go down there because if they stray off the path they are into the poison ivy and the ticks.''

Marguerite noticed that all the iced-tea glasses were empty. Sensing that they could all use another drink and that Officer Morgan could use a break to catch up on his notes, she paused and refilled the glasses, emptying the pitcher.

''I had better fix some more of this and set it outside to steep,'' she mused as she rinsed the pitcher.

''Not now, Marguerite! Continue with what happened,'' the chief urged somewhat testily.

''I walked down to the shed and it was locked. I couldn't understand that, as I never lock it. I usually just put the lock through the hasp to keep the door closed and I don't snap the lock. Rusty had followed me and was barking and scratching at the door. She never displays any interest in that shed, so I assumed some animal had gotten in there and that was what had gotten her so excited the night before. I had to go back to the cellar to get the key. Rusty stayed at the shed barking. I unlocked and opened the door hesitantly, expecting an animal to jump out. Nothing happened, so I stepped through the door and immediately noticed the smell. It is always musty in there, but not like this. It took me a little while to see clearly after coming in from the sunlight, but as soon as my eyes adjusted, I saw the body. Rusty was already walking around it sniffing and whining.'' Marguerite inwardly recoiled at the memory.

''Did either you or Rusty touch anything?''

''Not then. I ran out of the shed and pulled her out with me. When I got myself under control, I realized the person might be injured but alive and need help. So I went back in and closed the door behind me to keep out the dog. Then I felt for a pulse at the wrist and temple but couldn't find one. In fact, I'm not even sure I found the temple because the head was smashed. I left the shed again, closed the door, then noticed some dried blood on my hand. I wiped it off, locked the door, and called the police.''

Marguerite grimaced at her recollection of the blood and unconsciously wiped her hand on the side of her shorts.

"Did either you or Rusty remove anything from the scene? Think hard."

"No. Rusty was with me the whole time except when I went into the shed to check the pulse. But she was right outside the door barking and she returned to the house with me. She has not been out since then. I certainly didn't take anything from there. Except, of course, the little piece of paper I used to wipe my fingers."

"What piece of paper?" demanded the chief.

"It was only a small piece of paper outside the shed. I didn't want to wipe my hand on my clothes, so I picked it up and used it. It was outside," Marguerite emphasized defensively.

"What did you do with it?"

"I guess I threw it away."

"You mean you threw it away near the shed?" persisted the chief.

"No, I wouldn't do that. I never litter." Annoyed now.

"No need to get shirty with me, Marguerite. I'm just trying to help you remember. Try to recall your movements."

Somewhat mollified, Marguerite closed her eyes and tried to recapture the scene. "I came out of the shed, closed the door, discovered the caked blood on my fingers, looked around for a leaf to wipe them on, spotted the paper, used it, crumpled it in my hand, then what? I remember! I wanted to lock the shed, but I needed to use two hands, one to hold the lock steady and one to snap it closed. The paper was still in my hand, so I stuck it in my pocket."

Excited, Marguerite reached into her pocket and trium-

phantly withdrew a crumpled and dirtied piece of paper.
"Voilà!"

"Would you please repeat that last word, Ms. Smith?"
timidly interjected Officer Morgan, who had been furiously
trying to keep up with Marguerite's recital. This broke the
tension and brought smiles to their faces.

"V-O-I-L-À," patiently spelled the chief. "It's French."

Smoothing the piece of paper on the table, carefully using his handkerchief, the chief grumbled, "Of course, any
fingerprints on this won't be worth a damn after you
mauled it. Is this your handwriting?"

"No, it is not. And I have never seen that paper before.
It might have blown here."

"It might have. And it just might have been dropped by
the murderer."

"Or the victim," added Medeiros.

"Yes, or the victim. But what does it mean?"

The four of them stared at a series of numbers
and letters: *973.IPOH(E), 970.ICE(E), 970.IFEL(E),
948.GRA(O), 973.IGOL(O), 973.IMA(O)*.

"There is something familiar about those numbers, but
I just can't place it," puzzled Marguerite.

"If you remember what it is, call us," said Medeiros,
carefully placing the paper in a plastic evidence envelope.
"We'll send this to the lab along with the other evidence
the guys are collecting."

"Wait a minute, Al. I would like to have a list of those
numbers first. Morgan, copy that list into your notebook,"
ordered the chief.

Questioning temporarily over, the little group in the
kitchen went outdoors so that Marguerite could direct the
investigative team to the approximate area into which the
dog had run. From the back of the house they could see
Jeb, who had returned and was nervously pacing the patio
and smoking. Too impatient to await a table at the crowded

Clam Shack, he had opted for the takeout line and ordered a couple of hot dogs, which the boys were now munching. Jeb had remembered to raise the umbrellas over their chairs, a habit ingrained in him by Portia, who was vigilant against skin cancer and cringed at sunburned bodies.

Thinking of Portia reminded him that she would be calling in a couple of hours from Memphis, where she had gone on a business trip for her law firm. What would he tell her? As little as possible right now. No point in upsetting her when he did not know everything himself. Let it wait until tomorrow. In Jebediah's thirty-five years there had been many tomorrows for which he had waited. Of course, he knew it was never his judgment that was bad, only his luck.

Chapter Four

David Morgan, erstwhile painter, latter-day policeman, walked sluggishly beside Marguerite, both of them trailing Chief Nadeau, who was hurtling up the landscaped steps in a rush toward his car. He and Detective Medeiros had agreed that nothing more was to be learned at the scene for the moment and had decided to continue the investigation from police headquarters after the chief had radioed for an officer to interrogate the neighbors about events of the previous night and Medeiros had conferred with the forensic team.

"Got to get back to headquarters to see what kind of havoc the tourists are wreaking this weekend," were his parting words.

The "havoc" was unlikely to be anything that the officer-in-charge could not handle. But Frank Nadeau was a hands-on chief. Being on duty this summer Saturday, when his prerogative as chief could have assured him of duty-free weekends, was not accidental. In his first year as chief he tried absenting himself on weekends, planning to spend more time with his wife, who worked weekdays. But, typical of resort areas, most problems occurred on weekends, particularly in the summer. He could not ignore the call of the sirens, and his leisurely weekends were a sham. The next and subsequent summers he routinely worked weekends, taking off Wednesdays and Thursdays, and delighting in it. The beaches were less crowded, the fishing better, and the restaurants and theaters only relatively crowded.

As he drove the short distance to the new police headquarters, he pondered whether he had been too severe with Officer Morgan. His instructions to the young policeman had been to locate the Cape residence of Peter Dafoe; visit it to discover if any family members lived there with him, and if not, locate a colleague to immediately ID the body; seal the premises before leaving; and call the chief periodically with all pertinent information.

David Morgan had been stunned at this litany of charges and inquired weakly, "How do I find out where he lived?"

"You're a cop, Morgan! That's what cops do. They find out things." With that the chief turned on his heels and hurried to his car.

On reflection, he decided that no, he had not been too harsh. David had a good brain and a natural insight about people. Perhaps the latter was a trait of artists, never wanting to paint a photograph, preferring an X-ray image, a penetration of the surface. What he lacked was confidence. In two years of directing traffic, responding to accidents and complaints of barking dogs, he had never been intellectually challenged. This was the chance to test his mettle and discover if he had the potential he seemed at pains to subdue.

No fear of him messing up the investigation; Medeiros and Frank would be monitoring every move. Frank chuckled as he recalled his ingenuity in dropping this on David in Marguerite's presence. If anyone could shore up confidence and stir the imagination it was she, particularly if she considered herself a suspect. They were probably planning strategy right now, unsuspecting of his artful maneuver.

Frank was perceptive. David was already cheered by a cold ginger ale—the iced tea was gone—and a chicken salad sandwich with garden-fresh dill, testimony to Marguerite's aborted luncheon plans. Almost imperceptibly, Marguerite was making suggestions and attributing them to the officer.

"I think that is a great idea of yours, David," familiarly using his first name. "Start your inquiry at the National Seashore. If Peter Dafoe was excavating at Coast Guard Beach, the Seashore has to be involved. They probably have a record of everyone permitted on the site. You know how fussy they are."

Looking brighter now, the officer arose and wrapped the remaining half of his sandwich in a paper napkin. "You don't mind if I take it with me, do you, ma'am? I really want to get on this right away before their office closes." Without waiting for an answer, he eagerly hastened from the picnic table to his car, almost colliding with Johnny and Jamie, bored with the crime now that everyone had left. They ran up to Marguerite.

"Aunt Meg, you promised we could go to the beach. Dad won't take us. He says he doesn't feel well. Make him take us," winged Johnny.

"Jeb, are you ill?" she called to her nephew, still sitting on the patio smoking.

"A little, Aunt Marge. I told you I caught a bug somewhere. I'm not up to going to the beach. I think I should lie down a while."

"Aunt Meg, you take us," chorused the boys.

"Okay, we might as well go. It's late, but you won't be needing dinner until late because you just had lunch," replied Marguerite a little wearily. Aping Officer Morgan, she wrapped her own unfinished sandwich in a napkin and placed it, along with three peaches, in a plastic bag. Putting on her bathing suit was a matter of only a few minutes. Collecting the beach towels, a chair, sand buckets and shovels, and sunscreen, they were on their way. She was glad to be leaving behind the house and the horror enacted behind it and the uncharacteristically moody Jebediah, to be heading for the clean, clear, and hopefully cooler air of the late-afternoon beach, her favorite time of the day there. Amidst the squeals of tires and children, they were off.

The drive leading to the headquarters of the Cape Cod National Seashore was long and forked, with one tine leading to Marconi Beach and another to headquarters and Marconi Station, site of the first two-way transatlantic wireless message in 1903.

The Wellfleet oceanside beach was not a fortuitous location for such a venture, being windy and erosion prone, presenting unexpected challenges to Guglielmo Marconi, nurtured in the beneficent climes of Bologna and Rome. The first station was wrecked by a storm in 1901 before coming on line and had to be rebuilt for its historic message exchange between Theodore Roosevelt and Edward VII of England. The station was dismantled in 1920 and the ocean has claimed the site. Of the four original concrete bases, only the remains of two are still visible on the sand. It is appropriate that the bust of Marconi at the station is positioned with its back to the ocean.

David arrived in time to find the office open and, upon explaining his mission, a torrent of information was forthcoming. Yes, Dr. Peter Dafoe is the archaeologist in charge of the dig at Coast Guard Beach. They have found some amazing Native American artifacts, apparently very old. They may be the oldest evidences of Native American life on Cape Cod, and on and on went the ranger. Interesting though this was, David interrupted the flow, which threatened to become a deluge, and asked the pertinent question concerning a Cape Cod address for Dr. Dafoe.

"No, we only have his permanent address. The team members had to locate their own lodgings. We have so many summer workers to house that we have no room for them.''

''Do you have any idea which town he lives in?''

''No. No idea at all. But why don't you go down to the site? The other members of the team could tell you where he lives.''

''Will they be there now? On Saturday afternoon?''

The chief park ranger laughed. ''Saturday, Sunday, and holidays. These scientists work every day. They are racing to finish before bad weather stops them.''

''You mean cold weather?''

''No, cold weather doesn't stop them, either. But a hurricane or a northeaster could swamp the site. That's how it was uncovered in the first place.''

''Thanks for the help,'' said David, heading quickly for the door, cutting off the ranger's archaeological discourse.

Why isn't everything in life this peaceful? thought Marguerite, comfortably ensconced in a canvas beach chair, coolly shaded by its rooflike top, and contentedly munching her remaining half sandwich.

First Encounter Beach is a favorite of people with young children, because the water is calm and warmer than on the ocean side. The ebbing tide reveals shallows and rills and channels full of stranded sea creatures waiting timorously for the next flush of water. For beachgoers present at dead low tide, sand flats comprise the landscape as far as the eye can see and the legs can walk. Children dig and refill holes; splash and complain loudly of being splashed; run heedlessly about, then brake in panic looking for familiar faces; lose their pails and appropriate others; collect hermit crabs and proudly display them before fickly discarding them.

The homeliness of the scene belied the origin of the name. This was the site where the Pilgrims from the *May-*

flower first encountered the Indians. A group of Pilgrims, under the command of Captain Miles Standish, had landed on the beach and begun exploring the area when they hastily decamped amidst a shower of arrows from the direction of the trees.

There are several versions of the reason for the attack. It may have been the outcome of the food-short Pilgrims having located a store of corn on Corn Hill in Truro and absconding with it, heedless of the consequences to its owners. It may have been a fear of being captured and abducted by these white men as some of their brethren had been by earlier European visitors who fished in these waters. Or it may have been the primordial distrust and fear of strangers moving into one's neighborhood.

Marguerite's thoughts this sunny afternoon were absorbed by more proximate concerns triggered by observation of the two boys at play. James, the younger and fairer, had little-boy features that mirrored those of Portia at that age; John, darkly handsome already at eight years old, exhibited the grace and charm so irresistible in his father. Their personalities seemed to have been embedded in the genes that directed their physiognomies. John, decisive and confident, was always the leader, with his relaxed assumption of that role extending far beyond the seniority of his two-year age advantage over James. Poor James! Just like Portia—intelligent, introspective, and no match for the Newcomb clan.

Portia Fallon Newcomb was the only child of Marguerite's late brother, Denis, and his beloved and frail wife, Caroline. Denis, the poet of the Fallon family, yearned to be a great trial attorney and expound memorable thoughts on justice, liberty, and humanity, but his destiny was otherwise. Smitten by love while still in college, he married young and barely eked his way to graduation. In the days before guaranteed student loans, there was no way for him to attend law school except to work days and attend school at night, or to allow Caroline to support them. He refused to consider the latter and, after the birth of their daughter, increased living expenses and medical bills for Caroline forced him to abandon the former. Denis forsook his dream and became an insurance adjuster. But the romance of poetry lingered and he named his daughter Portia, the merger of his two loves—poetry and law.

Caroline died when Portia was ten years old; Denis, of a massive heart attack when she was eighteen and in her first year of college. Unromantic though a career in insurance was, it was one in which the employees were provided with the opportunity for extensive insurance coverage for themselves. Portia was momentarily stunned by this largesse, but she immediately invested it as she thought Denis would have wished. She transferred to Harvard University and continued on to Harvard Law School.

During Octoberfest of her final year in law school, she bumped into Jeb in Harvard Square; literally bumped into him and spilled her beer all over his Roots shirt, Orvis corduroys, and the Brooks Brothers sweater tied casually around his waist. Prepared to apologize profusely, she looked up at him and said—nothing. He took her breath away. Like generations of Fallons before her, she had ambiguous feelings about the Boston Brahmins, but this was the first one who had ever touched her. Jeb grasped her arms to prevent her from falling when they collided, and he had not let go. She grinned embarrassedly, mumbled a few senseless words. He ignored his sartorial damage and bought her another beer. They were married during spring break.

Though recruited by prestigious law firms, Portia ignored them and made a career of being Jeb's wife and the mother of two sons. Five years later, it became apparent that his career as president of the family business of ship chandlers might have lean days and she entered the job market, securing a position with a Boston law firm. Fortunately, she had made one concession to Marguerite, her closest relative, and had taken and passed the bar examination that first summer of her marriage. Now five years behind her law school peers, she was still a junior associate and likely to be selected for out-of-town assignments on summer weekends. One of the ironies of Portia's subordinate position was that her address was one of the best in Boston and the envy of even the senior partners. She and Jeb lived in the Newcomb mansion on Mt. Vernon Street near Louisburg Square in the Beacon Hill section. The house had been inherited by Jeb's mother, Mary Cinotti Newcomb, who hated both the house and the neighborhood and longed to sell after her husband died in 1985. A complicated estate and, to her mind, dilatory attorneys, prevented her from obtaining a clear title for two years. By that time the real estate market in Boston was soft, and Mary, comfortably settled in Virginia and with time and distance softening her views of Boston, removed the house from the market and allowed Jeb to rent it from her reasonably. Her sole proviso was that the rooms formerly occupied by her and her daughter, Lucia, remained available for their infrequent visits to Boston.

Marguerite was startled from her reverie by the crying James, rubbing his eyes with one hand and pointing accusingly to his brother with the other.

"He threw sand in my eyes," sobbed James.

"Let me look at it. But first stop rubbing it." Marguerite gently pulled his eyelid away from his eye and let his tears flush the sand, using the effects to heal the cause. With James quieted, Marguerite looked at her watch and noted that it was almost six o'clock.

"We have to get home, Jamie. Let's get Johnny."

Marguerite corraled both children and gathered up their

possessions, aided by the repentant John, first emptying the buckets of animal, vegetable, and mineral. Her tranquil interlude had ended. Back to the scene of the crime.

David Morgan was sweaty and sticky but optimistic on the drive to Coast Guard Beach. As predicted by the ranger, the archaeologists were at the dig. Trudging over the sand to reach them, his shoes filled with that grainy, abrasive irritant, but he resisted the temptation to remove his shoes and socks, judging it unsuitable to the dignity of his mission. His uniform, summerweight but fifty percent synthetic, was wet and clingy. How he longed to dive into the beckoning surf.

David had made several previous trips to the dig and was always surprised how they worked. Television documentaries of archaeological activity seemed to show areas under extensive excavation. This site was different. The only evidence of activity was a series of neatly marked holes, approximately one foot square, and a tape surrounding the entire perimeter instructing viewers to stay behind it. Very low-key—just like Cape Cod.

Hesitant to cross into the forbidden area, he called out to the nearest worker.

"Excuse me, please, but I would like to speak with the person in charge."

"Peter is in charge, but he's not here," answered a young man without lifting his head.

"Can I speak with you then?" persisted the officer.

"Sure, if it doesn't take too long. I want to finish this area before I leave," replied the tall, bespectacled young man as he approached.

Choosing his words carefully, David explained, "Dr. Dafoe has had an accident. We would like to know where he lives on the Cape and if any relatives live there with him."

Complacently, the young scientist inquired, "Did he drive into a pole? I wouldn't be surprised."

"No, it wasn't like that," responded David cautiously. "Now if you could give me the information I requested."

"Peter lives with me. I'm George O'Malley. Dell and Cynthia also live there."

"Are they here now?"

"Yes, they are right over there. Dell! Cynthia!" he called.

A young woman, her slenderness bordering emaciation, blondish hair pulled back in a ponytail, eyes squinting in the sun, turned and started toward them. Her petiteness was accentuated by the husky build of the young man who joined her. Dell was barely garbed in cutoff shorts and a tank top that strained against him, a look calculated to emphasize the musculature of the wearer.

The officer again offered the explanation of an accident and asked them to accompany him back to their house. Predictably, they all objected. They had work to finish. They could not leave yet. If Peter was in the hospital, there was nothing they could do for him. Surprised at their lack of concern and curiosity, David persisted in demanding they accompany him. As they grumblingly gathered their tools, he took the opportunity to obtain the names, addresses, and telephone numbers of the three other site workers.

Returning to the police cruiser, David radioed headquarters with his information, much to the relief of Medeiros, who had just completed a frustrating telephone conversation with a clerk in the personnel office at King's College. She was only a student working for the summer, she explained, and had no access to the personal files of staff members. Everyone else had gone home except for her and another student. No, she did not know the home telephone numbers of the personnel director or her assistant.

Cynthia and Dell drove their own cars while George went in the police car.

"This must be some accident if we all have to go," he muttered.

"Yes, it is. It's the worst accident he will ever have."

Chapter Five

The house to which George directed David was not a home but a summer cottage masquerading as a condominium. During the heated real estate market of the mid-1980s, some proprietors of summer cottage colonies, weary of the vagaries of tourism, had sold cottages as individual condominium units. In the chilly market of the 1990s, the disillusioned buyers discovered that the purported "good rental history" was a chimera and the cottages were apt to lie fallow many weeks. The archaeological team, under-funded and underpaid, was able to obtain affordable rates by renting for the season and doubling up—seven people in two cottages.

Dell, arriving first, opened the unlocked door and theatrically gestured in the policeman.

"Enter our humble abode," he intoned as he swept his arm outward.

The cottage could be seen all at once: two tiny bedrooms, a small living room, an eat-in kitchen, and a minimal bathroom. The unmatched furniture looked suspiciously like the random items available for the taking at the swap shop newly erected in the town disposal area.

David assembled everyone in the living room and bade them be seated. Sparing details, he apprised them of Dr. Dafoe's death, apparently murder, and keenly observed their reactions. Cynthia blanched and put her hand to her mouth, suppressing a cry. George abruptly jumped from his chair and grasped David by the arms.

"Who did it? How did it happen? Did it happen last night? He wasn't here this morning when we woke up," he cried all in one breath.

Dell showed no reaction at all. Either he was remarkably self-controlled, part of his machismo, or he was not surprised at the news. David made a mental note to watch him closely. Ignoring their questions, he introduced his own.

"Where does everyone sleep here?"

"Peter has, er, had the room to the right. As the big pooh-bah, he insisted on a room to himself. George and I share the other bedroom. Cynthia sleeps here. This is a studio couch," explained Dell. Noting David's questioning look at this last comment, he added, "I gallantly offered to let her share my room and put George out here."

"Are all of Dr. Dafoe's things in his room? Or are some of them in other areas of the house?"

Dell, the self-designated spokesman, answered again. "Everything is in his room. As you see, there is no storage space in this room. The other bedroom is crammed with George and me sharing it, and Cynthia keeps her clothes in there too. Peter was fussy about his room and even kept it locked with a key he found in the chest drawer. I am surprised it's open now. We only had one key for the front door, so it was easier to leave it open. But Peter always locked his door when he left. He said it was because he kept all the team's records in his room. He might have had a messy private life, but on a dig he was meticulous. Each of us kept a notebook, which he issued and collected daily. They are all in his room, because we were not able to get our notebooks this morning. We have each filled several of them."

Acutely aware of lacking a search warrant but convinced that looking in an open room was not the same as searching it, David addressed Dell, "Let's go and look in his room, but don't touch anything." As they started toward the bedroom, David queried, "By the way, what does Dell stand for?"

"Anthony." Dell grinned. "My mother objected to naming me Anthony because she cannot abide the nickname Tony. But my father insisted and inevitably people were calling me Tony. Mother was not to be thwarted, and if I was to have a nickname, she would choose it. So she started calling me Dell, for Della Robbia, my last name."

"Does everything in this room look the same?" asked David, nudging the partially opened door of Peter's bedroom.

Dell scanned the room slowly. "Yes, it looks the same. There are his reference books in the bookcase, including the published records of other digs in this area. The notebooks I mentioned are on the chest," declared Dell, pointing to a stack of twelve six-by-nine-and-a-half-inch spiral notebooks. "They are color-coded, yellow for Peter, blue for George, red for Cynthia, and purple for me. The colors prevented mix-ups, and he could locate one at a glance."

"Where are the notebooks for the other three members of your team?"

"You mean the kids? They are just undergraduate students participating in this for college credit. It actually costs them money to work with us. Each of us, except Peter, has one student assigned as an assistant. They don't originate any activity and don't keep the official records. Their assignment is to learn how a dig is organized and operates. It doesn't matter what we find. They are studying procedure and recording it all in their own diaries, from which they must write a term paper next month. Peter doesn't keep their diaries since they are not official records and belong to the students."

As Dell talked he continued to study the room, apparently looking for something. "There does seem to be something missing."

"What is missing?"

"The green notebook. Several times recently I saw Peter writing at night in a green notebook. There is no desk or table in here, so he was sitting on his bed with books spread around him, writing furiously in that notebook. I assumed he was preparing material for his classes in September, because all his notes for the dig were made in yellow notebooks. It surprised me because Peter tends to be a little casual about preparing lectures. They are brilliant but spontaneous. It's all up here," said Dell, pointing to his head.

"Maybe it's in one of the drawers," suggested David.

"Could be," agreed Dell.

Deciding that opening the drawers would be going too far, David noted that the closet door was ajar. Gingerly pushing it open using the tip of his foot, he scanned the contents without touching anything.

Dr. Dafoe traveled lightly. On hangers were two pairs of chinos, two pairs of shorts, a windbreaker, and a yellow oilskin mackintosh (did they work in the rain?). On the shelf lay a sweater and an oilskin hat. A loaded backpack, six or seven books, a tape recorder and tapes, a pair of brown leather work shoes, a half-filled laundry bag, and four opened packages of notebooks—yellow, blue, red, and purple, no green—were on the floor. Whatever else Peter had must be in the chest, which was off-limits for now. Beginning to feel skittish about being in this room, David quickly vacated it before inadvertently destroying any evidence.

"This bedroom must be sealed. Is there another key?"

"No. Peter had the only key," answered Cynthia, looking somewhat revived from her earlier shock.

"Does anyone have a key for the front door?" David asked.

"Yes, there is one in the drawer of the kitchen table. We rarely use it, because we have only one key for the four of us and there is nothing valuable in here anyway. Besides, the manager and his wife live in the house at the beginning of the driveway and keep their eyes on the whole establishment."

David had some yellow crime tape in his police car, but that would not seal a room. Someone would need to come down and install a padlock. But before he called for that he had a few more questions. The first order of business was to get some information on the three people present: names, addresses, phone numbers, and status on the archaeological team. They all were graduate students of archaeology at King's College in Cambridge. In fact, they were one-third of the total graduate students in archaeology.

"And not likely to increase in number any time soon," commented Cynthia.

"Why is that?" he asked, detecting the bitterness in Cynthia's voice.

"That's not for me to say. I'm only one of the peons here."

David deduced that Cynthia had a lot more to say, and he wanted to hear it. He would maneuver to separate her from the two men and try his question again. But for now he had other questions.

"Was Dr. Dafoe married?" he continued.

"That depends on what you mean by married," offered George, speaking for the first time since his outburst. "He is technically married to the gorgeous Jennifer, but they no longer share bed and board, not too often, that is. Peter camps out in a faculty studio apartment while Jennifer is comfortably boarded, and bedded I might add, in their Back Bay apartment. She refuses to live on campus or even in Cambridge. Too confining, she claims."

"Do you know her address?"

"No. I just know it is in Back Bay."

"I know where it is," offered Cynthia. As the three men turned to stare questioningly at her, she blushed and rushed to explain. "Peter asked me to pick up some mail that had been sent there. He knew I was going to be in the neighborhood that day."

David wrote the address and asked, "Did Dr. Dafoe have a car?"

"Yes, he did," answered Dell. "A blue Plymouth minivan. He liked to have a lot of room to transport people and supplies to a dig. Come to think of it, the car's not here. Was it found where he was murdered?"

"I don't know yet. Do you know the license plate number?"

"Yes," responded Dell and gave it to the officer.

Calling headquarters, David felt a stir of excitement, whether from the thrill of the hunt or the proximity of evil, he did not know.

The chief was perplexed, an unusual state for the decisive Frank Nadeau. Young Morgan was on his way to the morgue in Pocasset, accompanying Cynthia Williams, who had offered to identify the body. The two young men from the cottage were on their way to headquarters for questioning and would be joined later by Cynthia. A patrol car had been dispatched to the cottage before Morgan left, with orders to install a padlock on the bedroom, then pick up the three undergrads and take them to police headquarters.

Six people for questioning on a Saturday evening in July when all his officers would be needed for the expected weekend problems. The logical thing to do was to stay here and assist Medeiros with the questioning. But another thought was nagging at him. An estranged or semi-estranged wife in Boston. She had to be notified. Of course, they could contact the Boston police for this, but Frank wanted to be there when she was notified. *Cherchez la femme!* Though Frank's instinct whispered to him that this did not have the markings of a female crime, the possibility of a woman's involvement, perhaps with an accomplice, could not be disregarded.

Luckily, Sergeant Patterson was on duty tonight and he could work with Medeiros. The sergeant had spent ten years in the Washington, D.C., police force before abandoning the crime capital for a job on the Cape. It offered less money and less opportunity, but big benefits: a safe environment for his wife and children, and the likelihood of his living to collect a pension. He was the most experienced officer on the force in terms of familiarity with serious crime. The chief could also ask Officer Morgan to work a double shift to take up the slack. He was already past his quitting time and showed no impatience to leave.

Accustomed to making his own decisions, the chief chafed at the necessity to obtain the approval of Al Medeiros to make this trip. Al would probably want to question her himself, perhaps with Frank accompanying him. But there were at least six people to be questioned here, possibly more, involving many hours of work, and Mrs. Dafoe had to be notified quickly before learning of her husband's death from someone else. Frank had to be very convincing with Medeiros.

And he was. The chief was going to Boston. He would first call the Back Bay Area D station as a courtesy, and one of their officers would join him. Police were territorial and entered each other's backyards only after the formalities had been observed. He hoped someone he knew was the duty officer tonight. Frank did not let himself become isolated way out in Eastham. He scrupulously attended police seminars and conferences and was vice president of the Northeast Police Chiefs Association. His acquaintances among fellow police officials were numerous and extended from Providence to Portland and beyond.

Now that the easy problems were solved, he turned to the difficult one. Frank picked up the phone and dialed his wife.

As Marguerite approached her street upon returning from the beach, she noticed a police car and a flatbed truck in the school yard. The truck operator was attaching chains to a blue Plymouth minivan, preparatory to hauling it onto the tilted flatbed.

Even before Officer Morgan had called with the information about Peter Dafoe's car, Medeiros and Frank had reasoned that if the victim had been murdered where the body was found, as the evidence seemed to indicate, he might have driven to the vicinity in his own car. Frank called the Motor Vehicle Registry and obtained the car description and license plate number. He then radioed a car on patrol to search for the minivan on the streets surrounding the murder scene and, particularly, the school yard. The Plymouth had been spotted immediately.

The boys jumped out of the car almost before it stopped and ran toward the house.

"Don't go in the house," Marguerite called. "You're full of sand. Go down back to the outdoor shower and wash first."

As the boys ran to comply, Marguerite puzzled at the absence of barking. Rusty always greeted her return raucously. Entering the house, she called to Jeb and received no answer. She checked the bedrooms to see if he had fallen asleep—he really had appeared to be ill—but no Jeb and no rumpled bed. Because his car was still in the driveway, she knew he was nearby, perhaps walking the dog. How nearby became immediately evident as she heard Rusty's bark from the direction of the shed. Hurrying outside, she called, "Jeb! Rusty! Are you down there?"

Jeb peered out from the undergrowth in answer to her call and started to walk up the path, calling Rusty as he walked. But Rusty was not visible, having run farther into the woods and still barking, resisting Jeb's efforts to command her.

Marguerite was astonished at Rusty's tenacity and Jeb's temerity.

"Jeb, you are not supposed to be down there. The police have it taped off as a crime scene. They might still search it for evidence. We were distinctly told to stay away," she scolded.

"I know, Aunt Marge, but it wasn't my fault. Rusty wanted to go out, so I put her on a leash and walked her around the block. I took the leash off as we were entering the house and she ran down here. I just came down to get her," he explained sheepishly.

"She usually doesn't go into the woods because of the briars. There must be something attracting her. Rusty, come back here! Rusty!"

The dog resisted the call for a few more minutes, then appeared, moving slowly and dragging something beside her, a plastic Stop and Shop grocery bag. She dropped the bag in front of Marguerite, who gingerly opened it, removing an object carefully wrapped in cotton. Slowly peeling back the cotton, Marguerite revealed the upper portion of a skull, aged and blackened.

Horrified, she cried out, "Jeb, we must call the police."

And Jeb fainted.

Chapter Six

Cynthia needed no prodding during her ride to the morgue; she gushed with information. David fondly recollected his grandmother's favorite expression describing Philip, his gregarious younger brother: "You must have been vaccinated with a victrola needle." Cynthia was rambling in a stream-of-consciousness manner, seemingly unaware of the officer's presence.

"Peter had it all, but he threw it away. He was brilliant, came from money, went to the best schools, but never appreciated any of it. He tried marijuana in high school, alcohol in college, and cocaine in grad school. Liked them all. Still does—did. But he had two sides to him, the junkie side and the scholar side.

"His fieldwork was the best. He made a reputation while still a graduate student, assisting at a dig in Turkey that was not going well. He obtained a modern geological survey map of the area, compared it with old maps from Turkish archives, talked with villagers about their oral history, then hired a Jeep and drove around the site from all directions, without permission, of course. When he finished exploring, he told Dr. Potter, the chief archaeologist, that he was digging in the wrong place. The geography of the land and traditions of the people indicated that the ancient settlement was to the west of the present dig. Of course, Dr. Potter was furious and fired him, but that didn't bother

Peter. He always did what he wanted to do. Peter wired home for money and started his own dig to the west. He never bothered to get the approval of the Turkish authorities, and when he found the ruins exactly where he said they would be, he was arrested. Mommy flew to Turkey and in a three-way negotiation and the passing of baksheesh, the matter was resolved. The finds were considered part of the dig of Dr. Potter, who received the accolades. The artifacts were to remain in Turkey after being studied and photographed, and Peter was released from jail. He was in no hurry to leave Turkey, because he had met some hashish dealers while in jail and was having a merry old time. By the time he got back to Cambridge he was a folk hero and his reputation was made.

"It was always that way with Peter on a dig. He seemed to know exactly where to look, as if he could go back in time. He was fantastic to work with. But when it ended, he always went back to his old ways—alcohol or the drug of the day. I never knew anyone who could detox cold turkey for fieldwork and then start again as soon as the work was finished. I suspect that he was never really hooked on anything and was using his supposed addictions as a way of avoiding responsibilities. He even neglected to prepare completed work for publication once he returned home. Usually a graduate student assembled the manuscript from Peter's notes, which were voluminous.

"As bright as he was, he had difficulty getting a college teaching position because his reputation preceded him. Mrs. Dafoe pressured the trustees at King's College to lobby for him. Her father had been chairman of the board of trustees and the 'old boy network' was still strong—that and a couple of nice donations.

"Peter is the most popular lecturer in the department and his classes are always oversubscribed. But he is . . . was unreliable and worked in fits and starts. Thought grades were ridiculous, it's knowledge that counts, and had to be constantly goaded to give grades, usually late. Of course he never made professor and was never granted tenure. Never would have, either. Dr. Branowski hated him but feared his connections so he kept him on; a brilliant, aging hippie with no future. What a waste!''

Cynthia finally paused. The catharsis wearied her; she closed her eyes and leaned back against the headrest. David was disinclined to end the conversation.

''What about his wife?''

Enervated, Cynthia was slow to respond.

''Ah, yes, Jennifer. Peter had to have her because she was much sought after and would be his most beautiful trophy. Jennifer married him for the prominence of his family and the security of his money. In the end, neither got anything.''

''I would say she got what she wanted,'' suggested David.

''Wrong!'' said Cynthia. ''His name was not enough to secure him a professorship. He was tolerated but not savored at King's College. When Mommy died he was likely to lose even that tolerance. The money was not there, either. His father left everything to Peter's mother because of Peter's lifestyle. She keeps him on a pretty tight rein financially. She is always there to rescue him when absolutely necessary, but she does not give him a regular allowance. He lives on his salary and grants for fieldwork. Although most of his income goes to Jennifer, she has never been able to live in the lavish style she envisioned.''

''So Jennifer won't inherit anything?''

''That's a different matter. When they were newly married and Peter was frequently off on expeditions, he took out a large life insurance policy with Jennifer as the beneficiary. He evidently bragged about it, so it is generally known. She will probably get that.''

"Do you think he kept it? You said they were separated."

"Separated, but not divorced. My guess is that the policy is still in force or Jennifer would have split by now. She also takes pains to keep her dalliances secret. As long as she was discreet, Peter would never divorce her. He was still in love!"

Her discourse on Jennifer was interrupted by their arrival at the Barnstable County Hospital in Pocasset, site of the morgue to which Peter's body had been taken. David parked and walked around the car to coax the now subdued and hesitant Cynthia to perform that role for which she had so unthinkingly volunteered.

Never had Marguerite sipped a gin and tonic with more relish. She had earned it, she really had. Today had been the worst day of her life, worse even than the day Joe had told her he was leaving her for another woman. She had known about his affair for months and had been waiting for the other shoe to drop. It was almost with relief that she greeted his news. Anxiety protracted is anxiety compounded.

But nothing had prepared her for today: not years of urban living, not years of urban teaching and watching violence encroach upon the sanctity of schools, not even the nightly news with its litany of crime. She had been unscathed by such turbulence and was outraged that it had touched her in this most peaceful of places. Marguerite was reminded of John O'Hara's work *Appointment in Samarra*. One cannot outrun fate, because it is carried within us.

As for Jeb's behavior—what could she deduce from it? She knew he was not the best helpmate in a crisis, but fainting like that! He must really have been ill rather than malingering as she had suspected. Well, all was calm now. Jeb had been restored to consciousness in time to answer

Portia's call and offer his abbreviated version of the day's adventures, to which she had responded fearfully by demanding that he pack up the boys and Aunt Meg and return to Boston immediately. Jeb had countered weakly that Aunt Marge would never agree (he didn't ask her) and he had to stay to take care of her. Marguerite silently wondered as she heard this last comment. Who was taking care of whom? Eventually it was agreed that he would stay one more night and leave late Sunday, preferably with Aunt Marge. Marguerite had no intention of accompanying him, but she delayed that confrontation for the moment.

Jeb sat across from her on the deck, shaded now that the sun was on the other side of the house, drinking his gin and tonic rather more quickly than she. Dinner was cooking and occasionally blazing on the grill, ostensibly under the control of the two boys, who competitively turned the sausages more than necessary. Jeb and Marguerite munched on smoked trout spread along with their drinks. Luckily, she had prepared this on Friday, expecting them for dinner that evening. A bit of trout from the local smokehouse, macerated in a food processor with cream cheese and a dash of lemon juice. Wonderful on a cracker or a bagel chip with a couple of capers on top.

Jeb ate absentmindedly; Marguerite pleasurably. Life let you down, husbands and children let you down, but good food never did. The ten extra pounds that had crept on through the years testified to her conviction.

As she nibbled on trout and reveled in the cool evening breeze, she could not resist an occasional glance into the house in the direction of the locked cabinet holding the skull unearthed by the dog and now guarded from her urge to gnaw. Marguerite had called Chief Nadeau as soon as Jeb was on his feet, only to be informed that the chief had gone to Boston. Next she asked to speak with Detective Medeiros and was told that he was busy with questioning and could not be disturbed. Uncertain of the relationship but convinced of the skull's connection with the grisly murder, she wanted its disquieting presence removed from her home. Therefore, she described her discovery to the dispatcher and requested that someone come to remove it. The excited dispatcher instructed her not to touch it and to leave it as it was found. Too late for that, as it had been opened, examined, closed, and locked in a cabinet; but no need to convey this news. A police car would be around as soon as a minor accident on Route 6 was cleared.

A larger than usual flareup returned Marguerite's attention to the dinner. The sausages would soon be cremated if not served. She turned off the flame and closed the top of the grill to retain the heat, then hurried inside to put the corn in the boiling water. Potato salad, yellowed with hard-boiled eggs, and a plate of sliced native tomatoes topped with her garden basil completed the simple meal. Johnny and Jamie ate with an appetite abetted by their beach excursion, the novelty of an outdoor dinner, and their pride as chefs.

Marguerite longed to discuss the murder but suppressed that desire and backpedaled any mention of it by the boys. The latter was easier than expected. At ages six and eight, self-gratification was foremost and they were mostly concerned about what they would do next.

"Dad, can we play miniature golf?" inquired Johnny.

"Can we, Dad?" echoed Jamie.

"It is getting a little late," answered Jeb. "And we have to help Aunt Marge clear up."

"I'll do that, Jeb. There's nothing to it, just putting the dishes in the dishwasher. It might `be a good idea to go out," she urged, hoping to keep the boys occupied with thoughts other than those of murder. Besides, she was emotionally exhausted and wanted nothing more than to get rid of that skull, put her feet up, and think. She had to think this through before she went to bed or there would be no sleeping tonight.

Chief Nadeau rang the doorbell for the third time. He knew Mrs. Dafoe was at home, having been assured so by the Boston police officer accompanying him. Frank tactfully refrained from asking how he knew but was certain the information was correct. Besides, there were lights on and music playing in the second-floor apartment of the brownstone, once a single-family residence, now three apartments. Officer Gallagher impatiently placed his finger on the buzzer and left it there.

"That will get her down here."

He was right. Almost immediately, they heard someone running down the stairs and unlocking the door. Frank had contacted his office upon arriving at Back Bay Police Station and was given an outline of David Morgan's seventhirty P.M. call to headquarters from the morgue, cuing him to a beautiful wife with a large insurance policy. But no one had prepared him for Jennifer D'Amato Dafoe. Frank didn't know what an archaeologist's wife should look like, but no one's wife looked like this. Five feet eight inches tall; long blond hair that owed more to Clairol than to nature but who cared?; eyes a surreal violet; a figure slender and sleek at the same time, garbed in an exercise suit of hot pink and cool blue that ended in the high-cut bottom minus the usual black tights; and bare feet.

Her initial look of annoyance turned to the look of astonishment people acquire when recognizing their callers as police officers.

"Mrs. Dafoe?" asked Frank.

"Yes, I'm Jennifer Dafoe," the voice not consistent with the beauty of its bearer.

"I'm Chief Nadeau of Eastham and this is Officer Gallagher of Boston. May we come in?"

"I'm a little busy right now. Is there something I can help you with? Was my car stolen?"

"No, it is not about your car. It's about your husband. We would like to come in first," persisted the chief.

"Okay, but let me go ahead of you. I was exercising and have mats on the floor. I don't want you to trip on them."

With that she ran quickly up the stairs and closed the apartment door behind her. The two policemen followed more slowly and paused at the closed door. Sounds of activity were followed by sudden quiet, then the sound and motion of the opening door.

"Come in, please. What has Peter done now?" she inquired in the tone of a long-suffering wife.

"I'm afraid we have some bad news for you, Mrs. Dafoe. Your husband has been assaulted."

"Where? Is he badly hurt?"

"Yes, Mrs. Dafoe. He's dead."

Jennifer, only mildly interested up to now, started at the news and covered her mouth with her hand in the ages-old response to distress. William Gallagher went into the kitchen and returned with a glass of water, whether for drinking or resuscitation, he was not sure.

"But how did it happen? Was he in a fight? Peter didn't get into fights. He must have been mugged. Do people get mugged on the Cape? I didn't think so." As she asked and answered her own questions, the policemen waited patiently for her to assimilate the news. Finally running out of speculations, she turned to Frank, those incredible eyes wide open and focused directly on his, and in a softer voice said, "Tell me what happened."

The two men sat down on chairs across from the white leather couch on which Jennifer was seated, and Frank began.

"We don't know yet who did it or why. He appears to have been murdered, struck with a blunt object. His body was found this morning by the woman who owns the shed in which he was hidden, but the murder occurred last night. Do—''

Jennifer stopped him, eyes flaring. ''What woman?''

''Her name is Marguerite Smith. She lives in Eastham and does not seem to have known your husband.''

''That name is familiar,'' said Jennifer, concentrating. ''Wait a minute! I know who she is. That's Jeb Newcomb's aunt, actually his wife's aunt. Portia has no other relatives and is very close to her.''

The chief was startled at this news. He needed time to digest this bombshell but had to pursue the questioning.

''How do you know Jeb?''

''I met him at Harvard Business School,'' she answered coyly.

Incredulous at this last news, Frank asked, ''Did you attend Harvard Business School?''

Jennifer laughed, a harsh sound emanating from a smooth throat. ''Shocked, aren't you?'' She paused, but before Frank could think of anything to say, she continued, ''I didn't go there. I was the secretary to the head of the economics department. Just a kid on my first job. Jeb went to school there and started hanging around the office to talk to me.''

''Did he do more than talk to you?''

''What do you think?''

Frank ducked this question and asked, ''Were you serious about each other?''

''I was, Jeb wasn't. Simple as that.''

''Did Jeb know your husband?''

''He did after I married Peter. We ran into Jeb quite often. Cambridge is a smaller town than you think. Especially if you move in the college circles as they did at that time.''

Frank decided to pursue another avenue. ''Mrs. Dafoe,

do you know anyone who had a reason to kill your husband?''

''No. Not unless you count Dr. Branowski.''

''Who is Dr. Branowski?''

''The head of the archaeology department. Hated Peter with a passion. And that wife of his! Nearly choked on her spit every time she had to talk to me. Would have looked down her nose at me, but she was too short. That was one of the reasons I moved out of Cambridge. I couldn't hack it with those campus snobs,'' she recounted, still smarting from the memory.

''Let's get back to Dr. Branowski. Why did he hate Peter?''

''Because Peter was smarter than he was. Oh, Walter knew all the right people, married the right woman, and did all the right things. Even got to be head of the department. But he couldn't hide his mediocrity. Peter called him a dull plodder who knew all the right apples to polish. And of course his wife, stuck-up Pamela, helped. She set up all the apples for him. Peter was ten times smarter and could show him up any time he wanted. But mostly he didn't want to. Peter had no ambition and bad habits. Branowski probably lived in fear that Peter would clean up his act and try for the job. He had connections too—better than Mrs. Branowski's,'' she said proudly, protective now of Peter.

''Mrs. Dafoe, where were you last night from eight P.M. on?'' he suddenly asked, then just as suddenly stopped her from answering and advised her of her rights.

''Do you think I had anything to do with Peter's death?''

''I have to ask that of everyone,'' he explained, avoiding a direct answer.

''I was right here all night,'' she answered, chin upthrust.

''Was anyone with you? Did you call anyone or receive any phone calls?''

"No, no calls. No one was here." Jennifer looked frightened now.

"Think hard, Mrs. Dafoe. Is there anyone who can verify that you were here all night?"

A pause, a sigh from Jennifer, but no answer. She no longer looked into Frank's eyes but looked around the room as if searching for an answer. The answer came with an abrupt opening of the bedroom door and a masculine voice proclaiming, "I can verify it. She was here all night with me."

Chapter Seven

Red-eyed, pale-faced, and weak-kneed, Cynthia was led from the postmortem theater by David, nearly as pale-faced and weak-kneed as she. The body they had viewed was in the condition in which it had been found, the head befouled with caked blood, every corpuscle of which seemed to be revealed under the relentless overhead lights.

Dr. Mann, the medical examiner, was loathe to permit identification until the autopsy was completed and the deceased was in a condition and location more suitable for civilian sensibilities. However, resigned to the exigencies of police investigations, he hastily covered the body and admitted the young woman and the police officer, signaling the morgue attendant to be prepared for emergency. The doctor carefully lifted the sheet, revealing just the face.

Cynthia sobbed, ''Peter, Peter,'' and attempted to touch him, but was prevented from doing so by the attendant, alert to preserve the evidence.

Crying copiously, Cynthia offered no resistance to the pressure on her arm as David directed her from the room to a faux leather couch he had observed in the hallway. Leaving her to her grief, he went into the office and phoned Eastham headquarters with the information of the positive identification and an abbreviated version of his conversation with Cynthia concerning Mrs. Dafoe.

Feeling somewhat recovered, he returned to Cynthia,

59

who looked more than ever like a frail waif, and awkwardly thrust in front of her a handful of tissues taken from a box left thoughtfully on the desk. She accepted them word-lessly, dabbed eyes and nose and sat motionlessly, her tanned, skinny legs protruding from baggy shorts and end-ing incongruously in heavy work shoes, the entire costume almost comical in contrast to the solemn circumstances.

David noted that it was seven-thirty P.M. and a long time since that chicken salad sandwich at Marguerite's house. Ashamed to mention food in light of Cynthia's distress, he decided to drive to the nearest hamburger stand on the pre-text of getting coffee for her and hope that the aromas would entice her to eat. His healthy young appetite needed no such inducement.

Exiting the morgue, David considered the options. This was a hospital and probably had a cafeteria, but a hospital cafeteria was innately depressing and not likely to lift Cyn-thia's spirits. Better stick to his idea of a hamburger stand, but where? He had to find one before he got to Route 6, because there were no restaurants on it, only highway all the way to Eastham. The dilemma solved by an inquiry to a passing attendant, David drove from the hospital grounds to a nearby hamburger–pizza–fried clams–ice cream stand.

Leaving Cynthia seated at an outdoor picnic table, he ordered two hamburgers, two coffees, and a large order of fries. Gratefully, she grasped the coffee and took a large swallow. He noted goose bumps on her bare arms, either from shock or the cooling air or a synergy of both. Retriev-ing a sweater from the trunk of his cruiser, he handed it to her and she slipped it on. Although David was himself slen-der and of medium height, the sweater dwarfed Cynthia, who rolled up a sleeve in order to lift her coffee cup. In-advertently, he smiled; unconsciously, she smiled back, and the gloom lifted.

Tentatively, she nibbled at the hamburger, found it to her

liking, and sampled a few french fries. In a remarkably short time they were finished and on their way.

Reluctant to ask questions but eager to seize the opportunity, David opted to query her about the implications of the murder on the continuation of the dig.

"What will happen to the dig at the beach now? Will it close down or will they send someone else to be in charge?"

"Neither. The dig will go on, because although the grant was obtained by Peter, it was in the name of the college. This will only mean paperwork to obtain permission to delete Peter's name and substitute another. As for sending someone else, I doubt it. We have been working at the site for almost two months now, and anyone new would be unfamiliar with it. Besides, any archaeologist worth his salt is already engaged. They will just put one of the team in charge for the rest of the season, subject to the great Branowski's oversight, of course."

This was the second time David had detected her bitterness toward Dr. Branowski. He must pursue that subject, but first he asked, "Which of you is likely to be put in charge? Will it be you?"

"Me?" She laughed derisively. "Not likely. Anyone as poor as I am is invisible to Dr. Branowski. I'm older than the others. I had to work a few years after college to help my family. I'm just about making ends meet. It will probably be Dell."

"Dell! You mean Muscles?"

"Don't let his Rocky image fool you. Dell is the brightest one on the team next to Peter. I guess he's the brightest now," she remembered sadly. David waited for her to continue. "In fact, he'll probably be given Peter's teaching position too."

"Isn't he still a graduate student?" David asked.

"Yes, but not for long. His course work is finished and

he even has his thesis completed. He only has to defend it before the committee, but that will be a cinch for him. The oral is scheduled for September. He could have done it last fall, but he was on fieldwork in Arizona and had this planned for the summer. He should have his doctorate this fall with no trouble. Besides, he can teach classes without it. He already has a master's in archaeology.''

''So Dell stands to benefit from Peter's death.''

''If you put it that way, I guess he does,'' agreed Cynthia.

''Tell me about Dr. Branowski,'' David urged.

''There is not much to tell. He is a politician in a scholar's job. His work is good but undistinguished. Tends to play it safe, never rocks the boat, and is suspicious of anyone who does. Married above himself and is still climbing. Caters to students and professors with money and/or influence. Ignores everyone else, like me.''

''He will probably be relieved to be rid of Dr. Dafoe.''

''Yes, I expect he will. But I don't want to talk anymore. I'm exhausted.''

With that she closed her eyes, rested her head, and concluded their conversation.

The investigation was on hold, interrupted by the necessity for human sustenance. Officer Morgan's call to headquarters had temporarily halted the momentum of questioning and caused Medeiros to reflect. It was seven-thirty P.M. and he had not eaten since some time after noon, when he had hastily devoured a chili dog on the way to his car after being called from the Harwich fair. And how about those scientists? Who knows when they last ate? There was to be no question of mistreatment of persons in any of his cases; he had to be sure they were fed. In fact, he would even let them select their dinner, as long as it came between two pieces of bread from the delicatessen counter of the nearby Eastham Market.

When the food arrived, Medeiros assured himself that Sergeant Patterson had settled himself to eat in the same room as Dell and George to pick up any snippets of information inadvertently dropped and, principally, to prevent their comparing notes. Medeiros closed himself in the chief's office to think while he ate and to reconstruct what he had learned thus far.

The three undergraduate students had been questioned first, as he had guessed they were only at the periphery of the investigation. He seemed to have guessed correctly. They alibied each other. On Friday, everyone had left the dig at about six P.M. They all returned to the cottages in Peter's van and the three students went directly to their cottage, where they showered, dressed, and went out at about seven o'clock in Joshua's old Mustang.

Medeiros smiled as he reviewed their names: Joshua Cohen, Warren Chang, and Donna Jackson. It was not by chance. According to Warren, he had been recruited by the archaeology department when he was a freshman with no clear direction but probably bound for one of the traditional professions—business, law, medicine. Archaeology was one of the last professions still dominated by male Caucasians and the department wanted to diversify on its own terms and through its own selections; hence the courting of undergrads with superior academic standing, like Warren Chang and Donna Jackson, who was African-American.

The students drove to Provincetown and scurried onto the wharf parking lot just before the red light signaled a full lot. Dinner was a casual and cheap affair, garnered from the stands near the wharf. Joshua had a clam roll; Warren, a hot dog and french fries; Donna, two slices of pizza; all of it washed down with colas, the sine qua non of young diners. The hastily dispatched meal was followed by a walk down Commercial Street, already crowded with weekend arrivals. The walk was long and welcomed by muscles cramped from a day of stooping and bending.

On their return walk they stopped in the Captain Standish, where Joshua and Warren settled themselves at a table with a chessboard and engaged in their favorite warfare for about an hour and a half, interrupted occasionally by the waitress asking for their IDs and their orders, a total of two beers each and a lot of stalling. Donna sat with them for a while, then walked up to the bar and, in her words, made a fool of herself with the karaoke. She was sure someone would remember her. They left Provincetown at ten-thirty and were home about eleven P.M., watched the news on a snowy TV, and went to bed. No TGIF for them. Saturday was a working day.

Questioned separately, they all gave the same sequence. Unless the murder occurred at the latest time estimate— one A.M.—they were all clear. Medeiros was fairly certain that the doc had stretched that time frame to cover all eventualities and that the murder had occurred earlier, probably sometime around when the dog had been acting strangely. In any event, even assuming a one A.M. murder, these kids were together until eleven-thirty, and one of them could not have safely slipped away from the close quarters of their cottage for at least another hour, twelve-thirty A.M. That was very close to the maximum time frame for the murder. Starting the car was another risky factor, as it was parked behind the cottage, near the bedroom window. No, one of them could not have done it unless they were all in on it. Not a very likely supposition, but he made a note to check with the bartender at the Captain Standish about Donna's karaoke performance and the waitress about the chess players.

The three students had been released and instructed to remain on the Cape and come in on Monday to sign their statements. Relieved to be finished with the questions but reluctant to leave the center of excitement, they walked slowly to Joshua's car and sat dismally in it for some time. Centermost in their conversation was the impact of the murder on their course project. Was it over? Was the summer wasted? How could they turn this misfortune into a successful scientific term paper? Too bad they were not English majors. It would make a wonderful story. All of which conjectures confirm that misery is relative.

Having all but eliminated the three youngsters either as possible suspects or as sources of information in this crime, Medeiros hoped that more help would be forthcoming from the three people who shared the cottage with Dr. Dafoe. He had chosen to question Dell and thus far had obtained nothing of value to his investigation. Unfamiliar with the extensive homicide experience of Sergeant Patterson, he had assigned him the interrogation of George, who, visibly frightened and spectacles askew, seemed an easier subject than the self-assured, muscle-bound Dell. He hoped Patterson was having better luck than he was.

Charles Patterson, five years in Eastham with nary a murder, relished the opportunity to put his experience to use, but he regretted the necessity for it in his adopted town. The sergeant was adept at the "good cop, bad cop" routine of questioning, but he required an associate. This was a solo and he had to choose one role or the other. Opting for the softer approach, he put the nervous George at ease by encouraging him to talk about his background. From George's words and Patterson's deductions, a portrait emerged.

George O'Malley, of Hoboken, New Jersey, had attended Our Lady of Grace Grammar School in Hoboken and Hudson Catholic High School in Jersey City. Although living in a city recently gentrified and inhabited by yuppies commuting to New York City, George's family were native Hobokenites of very modest means who could never have afforded to buy at its current value the house in which they lived and that had been occupied by O'Malleys for nearly one hundred years. Influenced by the frugality of his upbringing, George attended Rutgers, a state university, rather than strap himself with the large loan obligations that would have resulted from a private college. This was a fortuitous decision because, without a large debt to worry him, he was freer to select a career of his choice without financial considerations.

George had a natural affinity toward the life sciences and it had been generally assumed during his high school years that he would become a doctor. Naturally scholarly but physically ungainly and socially awkward, he had little success in human relationships, creating within him an ambiguity toward a career in medicine for which he did not feel temperamentally suited.

A freshman course in human origins solved his quandary, and he never looked back. Now a graduate student of archaeology at King's College, he hoped to spend his life on field expeditions, writing, and maybe later as a museum curator, but never as a professor. He related better to bones than to people.

Patterson then tackled the activities of Friday night. "When did you leave the beach on Friday?"

"About six o'clock."

"Did you leave by yourself?"

"No, we all left together. Peter insisted on being there when we worked so he could supervise our activities. When he decided to quit around six we all quit, especially since we had been driven there in his van."

"How did you get home?"

"We drove back in his minivan."

This confirmed the earlier statements of the three undergrads. Now to the divergent activities.

"Tell me what happened when you returned to the cottage."

"Donna, Joshua, and Warren went directly into their cottage, taking with them the material from the dig. We went into ours."

"Was the door locked?"

"No, it usually isn't in the daytime."

"Was Dr. Dafoe's room locked?"

"Yes. He always locks it when he goes out."

"Continue," urged the sergeant.

"Peter collected our notebooks, because none of us were planning to work on them that night, walked to his door, unlocked it, went in, and closed it behind him. Dell called out that he had first dibs on the shower, grabbed a towel, and ran in. Cynthia and I sat down in the living room and waited for Dell to come out of the bathroom. There wasn't anything in the house for dinner, so we decided to treat ourselves and go to The Landing for dinner. We had received our stipends that afternoon and were tired of sandwiches. Dell finished in the shower and Cynthia went in next, then I did. None of us took long to dress and we left the cottage about seven o'clock. Dell left before us and went off with his gym bag."

"Did he say where he was going?"

"No, but he didn't have to. He joined the Nautilus club as soon as we got here and he works out there every chance he gets. Afraid his muscles will fall apart, I guess," George added with a trace of sarcasm.

"How did Cynthia and you get to The Landing?"

"In her car. She has an old jalopy."

"What make?"

"I don't know. But it's brown and dented. Some rust too."

It was evident to Patterson that George had no interest in cars, but he asked anyway, "Do you have a car?"

"No, I do not."

"What do you do for transportation if you want to go somewhere without the others?"

"Usually I don't have to. Peter drives us to the dig, and Cynthia or Dell do whatever shopping we need to do. I don't go out much at night, but when I do, I can go with one of them, or, if I am not going far, I use my bicycle."

"Where is your bicycle?"

"At the cottage. I keep it chained to a tree. They laugh at me and remind me that I am not in Hoboken but in Cape Cod where it is safe. That's how much they know! I never experienced anyone I knew being murdered in Hoboken."

As if supplying an interjection to this last bitter comment, the door flew open and Joanne Carpenter, the police dispatcher, entered.

"Sergeant Patterson, I'm taking orders for dinner. What would you and the other gentleman want?" she asked, pad and pencil poised.

Patterson cursed inwardly. He hated to interrupt the flow of an interrogation. Hiding his dismay—after all, it was not Joanne's fault—he ordered an Italian grinder and a bag of Cape Cod potato chips. George ordered ham and cheese on a roll with mustard and a bottle of seltzer.

"There is coffee outside. Medeiros would like you to call him now."

The phone call advised Patterson that he and George were to join Dell, now in the waiting room, and he was not to leave them alone together while they ate. They were not to go into the lavatory together, either.

Chafing at his role as sitter, Patterson was relieved when the food came and gave them all something to do. He gleaned nothing from their conversation because there wasn't any.

The three diners barely glanced at a female officer who entered the building and went directly into the chief's office, now occupied by Medeiros, carrying a slightly tattered Stop and Shop plastic bag. She exited immediately and left the building. Almost on her heels, Medeiros threw open the office door and shouted, "Patterson, get in here with those two guys!"

Gathering the remains of their dinners, the three men entered the office and were startled by an unexpected sight. In the center of the desk, amidst the stripped-away sides of a plastic grocery bag and a quantity of cotton padding, sat a skull: old, blackened, and with a damaged cranium. Only the upper section was displayed; the lower jaw was missing.

Addressing Dell, Medeiros asked, "Have you ever seen this skull before?"

"No, never," answered Dell emphatically.

"How about you?" turning to George.

"No, me either."

"How can you both be so sure it isn't something from the dig? Do you mark the pieces?"

"We didn't find any skulls at the dig. It is a home site, not a burial ground," volunteered George.

"Perhaps Dr. Dafoe found an Indian skull and hid it from you."

"I doubt if Peter felt the need to hide something he found, because, as the scientist of record, he would have received credit for whatever was discovered. If he hid it from us, his find would have no verification," expounded George, speaking more easily now that the topic was archaeology.

Dell had been quietly circling the desk studying the skull from all sides, peering at it closely but not touching it. The three men gazed at him curiously. Finally, Dell broke the silence.

"Sorry to ruin your theory, Detective Medeiros, but that is not a Native American skull. It's Caucasian."

Chapter Eight

Marguerite's cleanup was a matter of minutes: food in the refrigerator, dishes in the dishwasher, corn husks and cobs in the compost bin, a few scraps for Rusty, who had wolfed her dinner in anticipation of such largesse, and only the corn pot to wash.

At long last she was alone. Really alone. A policewoman had come and taken the skull, removing that ominous presence. The house was still warm, so she turned on a floor fan, put her feet on a hassock, and softly patted Rusty while running through the day's events.

First, the question of why in her backyard? It apparently had nothing to do with a burglary gone awry. Her house had been unoccupied for almost three hours, and Rusty did not pose much of a threat. The police had checked all the doors and windows for attempted entry and found nothing. Burglary had to be ruled out unless it was an attempt foiled by her return home. That would not account for the skull though, and she was convinced the skull was significant. It did not account for the murder, either, unless one burglar had turned on his cohort.

Starting anew, she concluded that Dr. Dafoe had driven his own car alone or with the murderer, parked in the school yard, and walked to the woods under his own power. It was inconceivable that he was already dead or unconscious when the car was parked. Someone would have had to drag him from the car in the school yard—a busy place on a hot summer night with the children's playground and adult softball games—carry it across a road busy with Friday-night traffic past her house and a neighbor's house, and struggle down into the woods. Impossible!

There was another scenario, however. Suppose the murderer drove the victim's car down the lane past her house, pulled to the side of the road, and dragged the body directly into the woods from there. He would not have been visible from any house but took the chance of being spotted by a passerby, although there were not as many on this lane as on the main road. Once out of the car and into the woods, only the car would have been visible. Since the car was Dr. Dafoe's, it would not have concerned the killer. Then drive the car to the school yard, abandon it, and walk away. Would he have had blood on him? Probably. But in the dark it would not have mattered, because the roads were not lit and he could have walked unnoticed or been picked up by a confederate. She supposed the police were checking the car for fingerprints or other evidence of a dead body in it. No, not a dead body: an unconscious one. Marguerite just remembered that Frank had said the murder weapon was Neil's baseball bat from her shed.

She considered her original supposition. Dr. Dafoe walked there of his own volition, either with the murderer or alone, and encountered the murderer. But why? Another thought came to her. Perhaps he was fleeing from someone and ran haphazardly into her woods. That made more sense. Unless he had accidentally stumbled upon her path, he would have been running blindly through an area thick with briars. Perhaps some evidence of his flight remained, like a shred of clothes or a trace of skin or blood. That must have been what the forensic team had been looking for when she saw them searching the woods. One thing they had not searched for was a rabbit hole, cleverly covered by

Rusty. She smiled and patted Rusty a little harder as she thought of a dog's instinctive behavior outwitting the best efforts of modern forensic experts.

Marguerite felt vastly relieved now that she had decided the murderer had chased his victim onto her property. That the body was in her shed was an unfortunate circumstance and had nothing to do with her or her family. She must remember to keep that shed locked hereafter.

Marguerite arose from her brief rest, refreshed now that her uncertainties had abated, and prepared to take Rusty for a walk. She would have to continue this practice until the police removed that intrusive yellow tape. It was a nuisance, but they would both be the better for the increased activity. Frank's sly remark about Rusty had hit home; they were both a little overweight.

When she returned she would check the basement for a substitute clam pail and some digging implements, the ones in the shed now off-limits. Murder or not, she still had two boys to take clamming in the morning.

Very little surprises a policeman, and neither Frank Nadeau nor William Gallagher was surprised that someone was hiding in the bedroom. Jennifer's hurry up the stairs to close the door behind her, the sounds of frantic activity, the absence of sweat on someone supposedly exercising, the scent of perfume, and, for Gallagher, the sight of two still-wet wineglasses on the kitchen sideboard were manifestations of a visitor whom she wished to conceal.

As the speaker languidly emerged, the two men stared despite their previous certainty of his existence. Only slightly taller than Jennifer; with the same blond hair (probably from the same hair salon) worn long and combed back, but, now and then, falling forward to be elegantly thrust back; eyes too blue to be natural; slender but not skinny with a perfect balance of muscle and flesh; garbed in an outfit that exactly matched Jennifer's. They could have been twins, or Ken and Barbie in virtual reality. Seating himself on the sofa beside Jennifer and putting an arm protectively (possessively?) around her, he inquired in carefully measured tones, "What else do you need to know about last night?"

Frank cleared his throat and asked, "First, I would like to know who you are."

"I am Jason Moore."

"Where do you live?"

"Right upstairs."

The chief mentally raised his eyebrows but continued smoothly, "What do you do for a living, Mr. Moore?"

"I am an actor."

Not surprising, that news. His entrance had been theatrically gripping.

"Are you appearing in something now?"

"No, not right now. I am between shows."

"What shows are you between?"

"I don't know what my career has to do with Jennifer's whereabouts last night. I told you she was here with me."

Frank sensed that he had touched a nerve and prodded it. "It probably has nothing at all to do with our investigation, but we have to establish the identities of alibi witnesses. Now what shows did you say you were between?"

Resigned, Jason answered, "In June I appeared in a GBS revival at the American Repertory Theatre. That's George Bernard Shaw," he explained patronizingly.

Frank made no comment and continued looking at him with a querulous expression, waiting for the remainder of the answer.

"I expect to do some further shows there in the fall," Jason added.

"Expect?" inquired Frank. "Nothing definite?"

"Actors don't have civil service jobs. They have to audition for roles." The trained actor's voice rose a note higher.

Ignoring the intended slur, Frank continued calmly, "When you are between roles, do you have another source of income?"

"Yes, I do," answered Jason, volunteering nothing further.

"And what is this source of income?"

"I am associated with Julio's."

"What is Julio's?"

"Only one of the finest restaurants in Boston," exclaimed Jason, his voice betraying his peevishness at this line of questioning.

Unperturbed, Frank persisted, "Exactly what do you do at Julio's?"

"I am part of the service staff."

"You're a waiter." A statement not a question, neither expecting an answer nor receiving one.

With Jason's ego somewhat deflated, Frank returned to the question of alibis.

"I would like you to account for your time last night from six o'clock on," said Frank, notebook ready.

Sensing a more serious turn to the questioning, Jennifer and Jason held hands, a little frightened. Jason began the narrative.

"I was at the gym until shortly before seven o'clock."

"Did anyone see you there?"

"Of course. I am very well known there."

I bet you are, thought Frank.

"On my way home I stopped at a Chinese restaurant, Hunan Garden, and picked up some takeout for Jennifer and me. Then I came here and we stayed in for the rest of the night. Jennifer had rented a video and we watched that for a couple of hours."

"What video, and where did you rent it, Mrs. Dafoe?"

"It was *A Few Good Men* and I rented it at Express Video," answered Jennifer quickly.

Turning back to Jason, Frank asked, "Were you in this apartment all night or did you return upstairs?"

"I was here all night."

"Did you have any phone calls, visitors, or deliveries? Did anyone see or speak to you here last night?"

"No, only Jennifer," he declared, smiling tenderly at her as he answered.

"Mrs. Dafoe, do you have anything to add to Mr. Moore's story? Something he may have forgotten that would help to establish that both of you were here?"

"I can't think of anything," she answered, staring at Frank with those eyes in which one could drown. "Unless the ticket on my car would help."

"What ticket?"

"I was parked too close to the hydrant and received a ticket during the night. I took it off the car this morning. Wait, I'll get it for you." She returned quickly with a parking ticket and handed it to Frank. He glanced at it and observed that it was issued at ten P.M. That probably gave the car an alibi, but it didn't do much for J and J, as he was coming to think of them. He gave the ticket to Gallagher, who took down the pertinent information to be checked for validity.

"Just a couple of more questions, Mrs. Dafoe. Who pays the rent here?"

Startled at the change of direction, Jennifer answered warily, "My husband does, of course."

"Do you have a job?"

"Not a steady job. I sometimes teach a couple of aerobics classes—jazzercise."

"Now that your husband is dead, what are the financial consequences to you? Does he leave you well provided for?"

"Huh, not likely. That old bitch never gave him any money of his own. Not even after he was married. Liked to keep him on a leash. Of course, whenever he got in trouble she was quick to rescue him. I doubt if she will rescue me, though." The hardness of the voice transmogrified Jennifer. To Frank the too-blond hair became brassy, the eyes shifty, the skin coarse, the figure immoderate, the clothes garish.

Frank quickly switched his glance to Jason and caught him squeezing her hand tightly in an effort to stem her intemperance. It succeeded. The beautiful Jennifer reappeared.

"I'm just so upset about Peter, I really am not myself."

"Of course, Mrs. Dafoe. We won't take much more of your time. Did Dr. Dafoe keep his personal papers here? Things like bank statements, policies, a will, receipts?"

"No, he kept everything at his place in Cambridge. He didn't like to bother me with business details," she answered sweetly, lowering her eyes.

"Then I guess we shall find everything we need in his apartment. By the way, Mrs. Dafoe, if there is anything you need from that apartment, you will have to wait. The place has been sealed by the police."

Mouth agape, her answer was aborted by another squeeze of the hand.

After informing her when and where she would be able to corroborate the identification and claim the body, Frank thanked her for her help and left the apartment with Gallagher. Glancing at his watch, Frank puzzled his next move. It was approaching ten o'clock. He would dearly love to speak with the senior Mrs. Dafoe to get her version of the recent relationship of Jennifer and Peter Dafoe. However, Medeiros had arranged for her to be informed of her son's death at approximately the same time Frank was notifying Jennifer. The lady was elderly and had received a great shock. Peter was her only child. Better let the questions wait. Especially since she was not a likely suspect.

The little group at police headquarters stood mesmerized by Dell's announcement. George, who had been ruing the interruption of his meal, turned his attention to the skull and examined it much as Dell had while continuing to eat his ham and cheese sandwich.

"He's right. This is a Europoid skull, not an Amerindian," George concurred

"How can you be so certain?" asked Medeiros.

"Several reasons," answered Dell. "First, there is the shape of the skull. This one is dolichocephalic or mesaticephalic—it is difficult to tell without the lower jaw and accurate measurements—but it is longer from front to back than from right to left and also longer vertically than the typical Amerindian skull. Of course, the vertical length is difficult to judge accurately without the mandible, but the horizontal aspects are clear. Amerindian skulls are brachycephalic or round, as are Oriental skulls.

"If the mandible were present you would also be able to observe the straight, vertical jaw of Europoid or Caucasian types. The upper jaw, or maxilla, gives a hint of this vertical line, but with the mandible it would become clearer.

"Luckily, the upper incisors are in place. The North American Indians and Asiatics have shovel-shaped incisors. That is not the case with this skull. The incisors are not spatulate. Negroid types don't have spatulate incisors either, but in other aspects, this does not conform to a Negroid skull.

"The cheekbones are also higher than this in Amerindians. All in all, you can be pretty sure this is a Caucasian skull."

"Well, I'll be damned," exclaimed Patterson. "You're reading that skull like a book."

"It is a book, Sergeant; the history of human evolution."

"How about this break in the back? What can you tell us about that?" asked Medeiros.

"It's impossible to tell without extensive examination, and maybe not even then, whether the individual was struck while alive, possibly causing his death, or whether the skull was damaged later. By the looks of that damaged area, I can tell you that the break is not recent. Its location, centered on the suture of the occipital and parietal bones, is a likely spot for someone to have been hit on the back of the head. You may have the skull of a murder victim," replied Dell teasingly.

"I hope I don't have to solve it," groused Medeiros.

"Not likely," said Dell. "That skull looks pretty old. To accurately assess its age you would need carbon dating."

"Do either of you know any reason why Dr. Dafoe would have an interest in this skull?"

"None at all," volunteered George, finally finished eating and ready to join the discussion. "His interest here was solely on Native American life in the pre-Columbian era. He considered anything after that to be bastardized. A few years ago in another site on Coast Guard Beach, to the north of our present dig, artifacts were discovered that were estimated to be ten thousand years old. Peter was hopeful that our excavation was from the same or an even earlier era. Our material has not yet been dated."

"Thank you for your information. I think we had better finish your statements before it gets any later," stated Medeiros.

Marguerite had not long returned from walking the dog when she heard banging on her front door and a chirping of boys' voices. "Aunt Meg, it's us. Open the door."

It was testimony to the day's events that the door was locked. Johnny and Jamie almost fell in the door when she opened it, so anxious were they to tell about their golf game: whose shot went under the windmill on the first try, and who hit the ball right in the whale's mouth. Strange to tell, their scores were identical. Jeb had evidently kept score.

Marguerite shooed them into the bathroom to wash the ice cream from their faces—chocolate for both. As she supervised the cleanup, she heard Jeb suddenly running upstairs and into the bathroom, followed by the sound of vomiting.

Promising the boys they could watch one television show, but only after they changed into pajamas, she walked into the living room and encountered a pale Jeb slowly descending the stairs.

"Those two gin and tonics didn't mix well with the ice cream."

"No, I guess they didn't," agreed Marguerite, reflecting meanwhile that Jeb had always bragged about his cast-iron stomach. Uncertainty once again returned to plague her thoughts.

Chapter Nine

Medeiros carefully wrapped the skull and locked it in the evidence safe. Tomorrow he would personally deliver it to the state police laboratory in Boston while there to pursue the Boston-Cambridge connections in this investigation.

The more immediate task was Anthony Della Robbia, intelligent, articulate, confident, and wary. He answered the questions and offered nothing further, particularly about his private life. Medeiros sensed a dichotomy in this young man. Although only five foot eight in height, his muscular build made him appear larger. Looking and dressing like a bouncer, he spoke in a cultured manner when discussing professional matters, then quickly reverted to the slangy bravado speech more suggestive of a surfer than an archaeologist.

He had driven himself and George to headquarters in one of the original two-seater Ford Thunderbirds, expensively restored, but was wearing shorts tattered to an extent Medeiros had not seen since the hippie era. Mr. Della Robbia evidently had not decided who he was.

Before the dinner break, Medeiros established that Dell had worked at the dig until about six o'clock, ridden back to the cottage with the rest of the team in Peter's minivan, gone immediately into the shower, dressed, and left the cottage at about six-thirty. He had driven directly to the

Nautilus club in Eastham, where he had worked out in the gym, took a swim, dressed, ate at the club, and left there about nine o'clock.

Medeiros picked up the thread at this point.

"Where did you go when you left the Nautilus?"

"I stopped at Roy's."

"Did you see anyone you knew?"

"No one I knew when I went in."

Puzzled, Medeiros asked, "Would you please clarify that?"

"I met someone whom I did not know before but I knew by the time we left."

"Who was it you met?"

"Some chick."

"Did the chick have a name?" Medeiros asked patiently.

"Yeah, Rosemary."

"Rosemary who?"

"Just Rosemary. That's all I know."

"And where does Rosemary live?" persisted Medeiros.

"Wellfleet."

"Do you know where in Wellfleet?"

"No."

"Let's review this. The only person who knows where you were after nine o'clock was Rosemary with no last name who lives somewhere in Wellfleet."

"That's it."

"Did Rosemary have a car?"

"I'm not sure. She was there with some other chicks and I don't know who had the wheels."

"Did you leave Roy's with Rosemary at any time?"

"Yeah, we left about ten-fifteen, ten-thirty."

"Where did you go?"

"We went for a ride, then a walk on the beach."

"Which beach?"

"First Encounter."

"What was the tide?" quickly asked Medeiros.

"Low, but incoming." Dell grinned. "By the way, Officer, that was a cool question, but you forgot that I work at the beach all day and know the tides anyway."

Ignoring this taunt, Medeiros continued. "What time did you leave the beach?"

"About a quarter to twelve. Rosemary had to meet her friends at Roy's at midnight. Just like Cinderella."

"Did you go into Roy's with her?"

"No, but she asked me to wait while she went in to check if the chicks were still there. She looked in and then gave me the high sign, so I left."

"Where did you go then?"

"Back to the cottage for some shut-eye."

"What time did you get home?"

"A little after midnight."

"Did anyone see you come in?"

"No, everyone was sacked out."

"Everyone?" inquired Medeiros.

"Well, George and Cynthia were. Peter's door was closed and I assumed he was there."

"Mr. Della Robbia, do you know anyone who had a motive to kill Dr. Dafoe?"

"I'm not sure what constitutes a motive for murder," the more articulate Dell offered, pondering the question. "Were there people whom Peter annoyed or who would benefit from his death? Certainly. He had a wife who would not live with him, a department head who was immensely jealous of him, and even I stand to gain by his death. But to say these are motives for murder is insufficient. One needs not only a motive for murder but the weakness of character to convince oneself that this is the only way and that the murder is justified. That excludes me. I already have an offer to teach in sunny California with a promise of extensive fieldwork as soon as I get my doctorate. I'm not sure I even want Peter's job if it is offered to me. I lose my tan up here.''

Abruptly changing the subject, Medeiros asked, ''Tell me about Saturday morning.''

''Cynthia and George were in the kitchen having breakfast when I got up. Peter had not come out of his room, so we decided to call him. I knocked on the door and got no answer, then tried the knob. It was locked or maybe just stuck. The doors in that cottage are poorly fitted. George said to knock harder, because Peter had been drinking the night before. When I still got no answer I looked outside and saw that his van was missing, so I did not try to pull the door open.''

''What did you think happened?''

''Nothing. I thought he went out early, because his van was gone.''

''Was it unusual for him to leave in the morning before you?''

''Yes.''

''What did you do next?''

''George and I drove to the dig in my car. Cynthia took her car and said she had to stop first at the drugstore.''

''What did you think when Peter was not at the dig?''

''I thought he had something important to do and would come later.''

This seemed to Medeiros all the information likely to be obtained from Dell. He spent a few more minutes getting a description of Rosemary and the bartender at Roy's and the name of the university offering Dell a job, thanked him for his cooperation, and let him go.

In the other room, Sergeant Patterson was completing his questioning of George.

''You stated that Cynthia and you left the cottage about seven o'clock to drive to The Landing. When did you arrive there?''

"In about twenty minutes. Cynthia stopped for gas."

"Tell me what happened there."

"We were lucky and got a table right away. It's always crowded on Friday night, but the people ahead of us all wanted tables for four and there was a table for two available. We sat down and both ordered fish and chips. We had a beer while we waited. After we were there a while, Peter came in."

"What time was that?" interrupted Patterson.

"I am not sure, but we hadn't received our food yet. It might have been about twenty minutes after we arrived," George decided.

"That would be about seven-forty," concluded Patterson.

"That's about right, but I can't say if it's exactly right."

"Did Dr. Dafoe see you?"

"No, he walked right to the bar and did not look in our direction. There's a partition between the bar and the dining room," explained George.

"Go on."

"We got our dinners right after that and had another beer with them. As soon as we finished eating, we got the check and left."

"What time was that?"

"It must have been about eight-thirty, because I got home about eight-forty or eight forty-five. I remember looking at the kitchen clock and thinking I could catch a nine o'clock movie on television."

"Was anyone else home?"

"No."

"Did you see Dr. Dafoe as you left The Landing?"

"Yes, I did, and I was somewhat surprised. He was at the far end of the bar and I saw him pick up a beer and drink it. That was the first time I knew of him drinking since we started the dig."

"Did he see you?" asked Patterson.

"No, he was looking in the other direction."

"Who was he with?"

"I don't know. The bar was crowded and there were people near him, but I didn't know them and I'm not even sure if he was with any of them."

"Let's get back to you. When you returned home did Cynthia and you both watch television?"

"No, Cynthia didn't come in. After I got out of the car, she changed her mind and said she was going to drop over to Roy's for a while to listen to the music."

"Did she ask you to accompany her?"

"No. She knows I hate Roy's. Too noisy, too crowded, too smoky."

"So you went into the house without Cynthia. Tell me what you did."

"I turned on the television and, at nine o'clock, tried to find a good movie. There wasn't anything I liked, so I watched baseball for a while, but it made me sleepy. I guess the two beers helped too. At ten o'clock I went into my room with a book to read, but I did not read long and fell asleep. I must have fallen asleep right before Cynthia came home."

"When was that?"

"I'm not sure when she came in, but I was awakened by her hitting the bathroom door to open it. The door sticks sometimes. She couldn't open it, so I got up and went to help her. The light in the kitchen was on and I noticed it was ten forty-five."

"Had Cynthia just come in?"

"I don't think so. She was in her pajamas."

"Did she say anything about where she had been?"

"Only that Roy's was crowded as usual."

"What happened then?"

"I went back to bed. A few minutes later the kitchen

light was turned off and I heard Cynthia go into the living room.''

''Did you hear Dell come in?''

''No, I'm a pretty heavy sleeper and he is quiet if he comes in after I'm in bed.''

Sergeant Patterson's final questions concerned Saturday morning, and the answers were essentially the same as those given by Dell. George knew no one with a motive to murder Dr. Dafoe and was rather put out by the inconsiderateness of the murderer in interrupting an important scientific exploration.

George left the office and was relieved to discover Dell waiting for him. As they walked into the parking lot, Cynthia was emerging from a police cruiser. Looking wan and dispirited, she barely acknowledged their presence but followed David Morgan as if by rote.

Medeiros judged that her energy was expended and her reserves exhausted. Yet he could not let her go home without obtaining at least a preliminary statement. Offering her coffee, which she accepted, he led her into the chief's office and to the most comfortable chair as Sergeant Patterson sat himself unobtrusively behind her.

Cynthia's grief was treated with respect by Medeiros. Of all the people connected thus far with Dr. Dafoe, only she seemed to mourn him. In his own deeply religious, closely knit Portuguese community, everyone's passing was mourned. Peter Dafoe deserved no less.

Questioning her gently, he brought her up to the time when she drove George home and left him.

''Where did you go when you left George?''

''I drove over to Roy's''

''Did you go in?''

''Yes, I did.''

''Where were you seated?''

''At the bar.''

"Which bar?"

"The small bar by the pinball machines. The large bar was too crowded."

"Did you see anyone you know?"

"No one. I don't know many people here."

"Think hard. Was there anyone who looked even vaguely familiar?"

"No, no one."

"Was it crowded?"

"Yes, very crowded."

"From where you were seated could you see people at the other bar?"

"No, I could not."

"Could you see the dance floor?"

"Not too well. There were a lot of people standing around."

"Have you been to Roy's at other times?"

"Once or twice."

"Who was the musical group?" continued Medeiros.

"There was no group. It was a DJ."

"What time did you leave?"

"About ten-fifteen or ten-twenty."

"Did you go straight home?"

"Yes, I did."

"What did you do when you went home?"

"I changed into my pajamas and went into the kitchen to make a cup of tea. Then I decided I was too tired for tea and went into the bathroom to brush my teeth. The door stuck and I was hitting it to open it when George came out of his room and pushed it open from the outside. He went back to bed and I put out the kitchen light and went to bed also."

"Was Dr. Dafoe's room open or closed when you arrived home?"

"Closed," answered Cynthia wearily.

Medeiros' queries about Saturday morning revealed the same sequence of events as he had obtained from Dell. She confirmed leaving the cottage when they did but in her own car, and going to the drugstore before heading for the beach.

"Miss Williams, we are aware that you have had a traumatic day and wish to thank you for your assistance to us, particularly in identifying the body. It cannot have been easy for you. You may continue to live in the cottage, but Dr. Dafoe's room is locked and off-limits. We would also like all of you to lock the front door when the cottage is empty, at least until further notice."

Cynthia nodded her head mutely and once again followed David as if sleepwalking. She had never removed his sweater and he wanted it back, but he delayed asking for it until he pulled up to the cottage.

"What sweater?" she asked, numb now to reality.

For once, Frank relished the long drive home from Boston. It was late enough for the roads to be lightly traveled once he left the Hub, and the easy drive gave him time to meditate, a luxury he had lacked all that busy day.

J and J were obviously lovers—too obviously. David's encapsulated version of Cynthia's conversation had led Frank to believe that J female had distanced herself from her husband, but she wanted to remain married to him and, consequently, was very discreet. Then why had they remained in her apartment when Jason's was so conveniently located upstairs?

To be sure, Peter was busily engaged on Cape Cod, but there was nothing to prevent him from driving up in the evening. Why were they so confident? Did they know they had nothing to worry about because Peter was dead?

Neither of them had an independent alibi for any time after seven P.M., and Jennifer had none for even earlier than that. Eastham was a one-and-a-half to two-hour drive, depending on traffic (make it two hours on a Friday), which could place both in Eastham at nine o'clock. Even if they arrived later, they were well within the estimated time of the murder.

Priority number one was to check on an insurance policy. He had refrained from mentioning it to her, because he didn't want to get the wind up yet, and he noted that she had also avoided the issue. Check on death benefits from the college too.

Priority number two was the Motor Vehicle Registry. Jennifer's car is conveniently accounted for (was it deliberately left near a fire hydrant?), but did Mr. Moore own a car? While on the subject of Jason, he would like to check out his finances also. That was a pretty expensive neighborhood. Was he living at the end of his financial rope? Jennifer could be quite a catch as an heiress—all those looks and money too.

Of course, there was one more path to pursue in this mystery, and it was one that troubled him. Jennifer knew Jeb Newcomb and claimed he knew Peter. Why no mention of this? He was certain he had mentioned the name of the deceased to Jeb but would review Officer Morgan's notes to verify it. Another priority on his mental list.

Frank was pragmatic enough to know that all his speculations were a house of cards unless the forensic team came through with some hard evidence. Meanwhile, he would pursue the motive and the opportunity as they pursued the hair and fibers.

Marguerite was distraught, tired but too wired to sleep. Her mind would not let her body rest. Employing her customary solution to infrequent bouts of sleeplessness, she perused her latest cache of library books in an effort to choose the one most likely to bore her to sleep. The books were on the night stand with the spines facing her. Recognition struck her.

"I've got it," she said aloud to Rusty. "We must call Frank first thing in the morning."

Chapter Ten

Medeiros was on the road to Boston at seven A.M. Although morning traffic was usually light heading off-Cape on warm, sunny, beach Sundays, he did not intend to test it. Besides, this early trip gave him an excuse to breakfast on the way: bacon, eggs, and lots of buttered toast, maybe even a little jam, instead of the latest bran cereal promoted by his wife as sure to decrease his cholesterol. Cholesterol! His grandfather and father had two eggs for breakfast every day. Grandpa lived to ninety-three and Poppa was now a vigorous eighty. Bran is so boring, it just makes you think you are living longer.

His first destination was the state police laboratory in Boston to which he delivered the skull. What a case! The two probable witnesses to the murder are mute—a dog and a skull.

Accomplishing this errand with dispatch, Medeiros drove to the Cambridge police precinct for the key to the padlock they had placed on Peter Dafoe's apartment. A Cambridge police officer was assigned to accompany him for any needed assistance and to reseal the premises when they left.

With the privilege of uniform, he parked in a tow zone directly in front of the apartment house, momentarily pitying the people in cars circling for landing spots. He pushed a button at random to get buzzed into the building and mentally chastised the accommodating resident who so freely admitted an unknown bell pusher.

Armed with a search warrant, the officers entered Peter's apartment, a studio: one large sitting and bedroom, a galley kitchen, and a bathroom. Although reserved for faculty, the apartment had the same tired, just-passing-through look of student apartments. Scotch tape marks on the walls from previous tenants' posters, scuffed woodwork, badly plastered nail holes, paint of an indeterminate color, and a shower curtain drooping for lack of two hooks were testimony to the apathy of past and present occupants.

There was no attempt to disguise the room as a sitting room by installing a sofa bed. Dr. Dafoe slept on a futon with a platform, unashamedly occupying the center of the long wall. The furniture was an eclectic mix of Dafoe antiques and discards from former residents. Two easy chairs, one with silk brocade upholstery and the other with a patched leather seat and a matching patched footstool, sat companionably side by side, sharing a glass-stained, cigarette-burned table. The only other seating accommodation was a maple desk chair pulled up to a large Queen Anne mahogany table covered with books and papers.

Even a cursory glance revealed to Medeiros that the table's effects were not haphazardly strewn but precisely arranged. Each stack of books pertained to a specific subject and the adjacent papers and notebooks related to that topic. Peter had within arm's reach all his current archaeological interests.

The smallest pile, an outline of two pages, was headed *Field Archaeology* and hinted at the contents of the course he would have taught in September. Hinted was the requisite description, because of the absence of lecture notes, bibliography, or anything at all to add flesh to the skeletal outline. Dell's appraisal of Peter's cavalier attitude to class presentation was apparently accurate.

Perusing the titles of the books, Medeiros concluded that Peter had a predilection for Native American archaeology and anthropology, at least at the present time, he corrected himself, mindful of Peter's early experiences in Turkey. There was no clue as to the provenance of the curious Caucasian skull on Cape Cod.

Turning from the table, Medeiros went next to a cherry wood highboy of excellent lineage, standing incongruously beside the futon. He carefully examined the contents of each drawer and found nothing helpful, only clothes, cuff links, and tie pins of a more formal era, rolled-up diplomas, and the assorted mementos that define a life.

Puzzled as to the lack of personal papers, Medeiros opened the clothes closet and discovered an accordion envelope designed to organize one's personal papers. The interior was divided into compartments, the first group alphabetized A through Z, the second group headed with specific designations such as *Automobile, Bank Statements,* and so on.

Under *Automobiles,* Medeiros found the ownership certificates for the Plymouth minivan and a GMAC payment book for a Buick Saturn, evidently the one Jennifer was using. The bank statements revealed a very modest savings account and a checking account with a small balance. The insurance compartment was enigmatic. Peter had health insurance, a straight life insurance policy for twenty thousand dollars, and a policy from King's University entitling his beneficiary to a year's salary and the return of his pension contributions. These did not signal a motive for murder. Sifting further through the compartments, Medeiros found accumulated receipts for gas, electricity, phones, rent, clothes, and at last, for insurance premiums. Comparing the receipts with the policies, he isolated a few receipts from an insurance company for which he found no accompanying policy. The latest receipt was for June and satisfied the premium through December. A phone call to the company was a must for Monday morning.

The remaining contents of the apartment revealed little of interest to Medeiros, occupied as it was by bookcase after bookcase, assorted and ill-matched, some venerable antiques, others crudely knocked together of unpainted wood. He was struck as always by the pathos of possessions, so important to the living yet so trivial after death.

Taking only the accordion file with him after preparing a receipt for it witnessed by the Cambridge officer, Medeiros returned to his cruiser and locked the file in the trunk before driving back over the Charles River to Boston to interview the victim's mother.

Marguerite arose earlier than usual on Sunday morning, unrested and uneasy. Her antidote for anxiety was work, and today's schedule provided plenty of that. Glad for once of the early-rising habits of children, she occupied herself with preparing breakfast for John and James before brewing coffee for herself and Jeb, whom she heard showering. Resisting her efforts to serve them oatmeal, the boys held out for her homemade cranberry bread, which they had earlier espied. *At least I made it with whole-wheat flour*, she consoled herself, pouring orange juice. Tempted herself by the luscious berries and rich walnuts, she joined them when the coffee was ready and slathered cream cheese on hers, more lavishly than necessary. Apparently unable to breakfast without a cigarette, Jeb took his coffee out to the deck with only a single piece of toast. *No wonder he stays so trim,* thought Marguerite grudgingly.

Jeb still looked unwell, but Marguerite was insistent that he join the clam diggers. The fresh air would do him good; it was certainly better than sitting here smoking.

Clamming at Salt Pond was permitted only on Sunday and at a time regulated by the tide, this time posted weekly by the park rangers. It commenced today at eight-thirty A.M.

Marguerite had selected a pail and two shovels, garden trowels really, as substitutes for the clam pail and rakes, now locked uselessly in the shed. The shovels were a bow to caution: They would result in a lot of broken clams but would spare little fingers from the inevitable cuts inflicted by the aptly named razor clams. She dressed in old shorts and a sleeveless shirt with a pocket for her shellfish permit; the boys, once again, in their neon bathing suits. Jeb donned a bathing suit and topped it with a sun-faded T-shirt.

At eight o'clock Marguerite rang the chief at headquarters, anxious to tell him of her late-night inspiration.

"Frank, remember those numbers and letters on the piece of paper I found?"

"You mean the one you messed up?"

"I mean the one I saved for you. I think I know what they mean."

"Well, spit it out, Marguerite."

"They are library catalog numbers. The ones on the spine of every library book."

Frank hesitated, trying to recall the sequence of those numbers and letters. "I think you're right, but I'll have to get Morgan's notes to verify it. That was good thinking. *Merci.*"

"Il n'y a pas de quoi! Let me know how it works out, but don't call for an hour or two. We are going clamming at Salt Pond."

"Is Jeb going with you?"

"Yes, he is. Why do you ask?"

"I'd like to speak with him again. Would you ask him to come down to the station this morning?"

"Is anything wrong?"

"Just want to clarify a few things," hedged Frank. "Thanks again for the help with those numbers."

Troubled, Marguerite put down the phone slowly and turned to Jeb. "The chief would like you to drop over to the station this morning. He just wants to clarify a few things."

Jeb drew in his breath sharply but exhibited no other signs of concern. "I guess I had better do that now and get it over with. I'll change first. Don't want to go there in a bathing suit."

"Fine, Jeb. I'll take the boys. If you finish quickly, you can join us," she suggested, displaying a confidence she did not feel. "Let's go, boys! John, carry the pail; James, carry the shovels; and I'll take a couple of towels."

As he watched the little group marching down the driveway, Jeb came close to tears for the first time in his adult life.

Intruding on a mother's grief was distasteful to the sensibilities of Albert Medeiros, and he would have avoided it if he could. But he was an agent operating on behalf of the murder victim and he owed that victim an investigation devoid of personal considerations. He had little expectation of receiving from Mrs. Dafoe any information concerning the events of Friday night, but he had every expectation of learning something of Peter Dafoe, the man and the son. Dr. Dafoe, like all mankind, was the product of the genes, experiences, beliefs, memories, foibles, frivolities, and opinions of his ancestors, family, friends, and acquaintances. Unmask the victim and you may find the motive for his murder.

Medeiros emitted a surprised whistle as he located the address on Boylston Street. Expecting a venerable family home, he was staring at one of the luxury condominium buildings newly favored by the rich who no longer commanded the legions of servants requisite for maintenance of those cavernous and aging landmarks.

With even the illegal parking spaces filled, he pulled into the RESIDENTS ONLY garage and slid into one of the spaces reserved for management. The attendant, unenviably positioned between an irascible building manager and the unyielding arm of the law, stood transfixed, mouth moving but nothing coherent escaping.

"Keep an eye on that car," Medeiros called over his shoulder as he walked away chuckling to himself. *I bet that boy's rap sheet would be interesting*, he thought to himself, recognizing the particular look with which miscreants greet the law, a look not found on upstanding citizens.

Passing muster with the concierge, who phoned the apartment before admitting him to the elevator, Medeiros was whisked upstairs in a silent ride and received into the apartment by a uniformed maid.

Prepared for a decor featuring the companions to the few good pieces of furniture in Peter's apartment, he found instead an entry hall papered in grass cloth and devoid of furniture, featuring only an enormous free-form pottery vase bearing an arrangement of grasses and twisted, bare branches. Following the maid into a large sitting room, he found it to be decorated in white and beige of many shades and textures. The carpet was the palest of beiges; the sofa, a nubby white cotton fabric; the occasional chairs were upholstered in batik-dyed beiges, each one different but all coordinated. At the windows were the sheerest white curtains, moving even in the scant breeze of this summer morning.

Color was provided only by the accessories that could be changed at a whim or by the magic wand of the decorator. The paintings on the wall were confined to American Impressionists and included works by Frank Weston Benson, Edward Hamilton, Mary Cassatt, and Childe Hassam.

Although Medeiros did not recognize the paintings, he recognized the quality, having lived most of his life amidst the art colony in Provincetown. He silently speculated as to whether Mrs. Dafoe had a store of paintings that changed seasonally, perhaps some Rembrandts for winter or Van Goghs for springtime. Clear glass vases of modern design bearing fresh flowers were scattered about the large room, each arrangement containing flowers of a single color, accented by green leaves and dainty white baby's breath, and positioned so as to highlight the dominant color of a particular painting. The flower selections were in peach, yellow, and red. Additional splashes of color were provided by the carefully selected bowls, bookends, book jackets, mantle ornaments, and the brilliant print tablecloth on a small, round table placed near a window, the print echoed in the upholstery of two accompanying chairs. Only a heavy antique silver tea service on the table provided a corridor to the past.

His thoughts were interrupted by the entry of Mrs. Victoria Dafoe, and this provided the second surprise. Of medium height, slender, simply but elegantly coiffed with no gray visible, probably sixty-five but resisting it, and dressed in a pale blue cotton dress with the simple lines that only the most expensive clothes achieve, Mrs. Dafoe moved swiftly toward him and extended her hand.

"Thank you for coming, Detective Medeiros. I must know more about my dear Peter. Who did this to him? Do you have anyone under arrest?" She seemed remarkably calm and self-possessed for a grieving mother, but Medeiros supposed this was her public face, part of the Anglo tradition of "a stiff upper lip." He was certain no one dared call this woman Vicki.

"Mrs. Dafoe, I would like to express my sympathy for the loss of your son. I know this is an intrusion upon—"

"Yes. Yes, I know," interrupted Mrs. Dafoe, "but let

us proceed with the matter at hand. Tell me everything you know about this dreadful matter,'' she said, indicating a chair in which he should be seated. Medeiros sat in the armchair to which he was directed, thankful for the absence of those annoying little pillows women seemed to favor.

The roles had reversed and the questioner became the questionee as Medeiros compliantly recited the facts to this astonishingly poised woman.

"And whom do you suspect?"

"At this time, everyone and no one. We are questioning people who worked with him and others who knew him and could have been on the Cape. What we do not have yet is a motive. We don't think it was a random killing, but a deliberate one. I was hoping you could tell me something about your son that would provide a motive for his death."

"Humph," she grunted, her first departure from elegance. "You do not have to look far. Just check on that harlot he married. I told him she would be the ruination of him, but even I did not expect her to go this far."

"Why would she murder him? I understand he was devoted to her," inquired Medeiros ingenuously.

"Why? The usual reason girls like that marry someone above themselves. Money! She thought she would be living like this." Mrs. Dafoe swept her arms, indicating the apartment. "She was not aware that Peter had no money of his own, and she evidently did not have the patience to wait until I died. Come to think of it, I am surprised it was not me she murdered. She probably would have if she had been sure Peter would inherit unconditionally."

"But if Dr. Dafoe had no money to leave her, why would she kill him?"

"The insurance, that's why! Peter was a brilliant boy but foolish about Jennifer. He had a large insurance policy on his life with her as the beneficiary. I suppose it was his way of making that woman independent of me. I was always very generous with Peter, but when he married against my wishes, I refused to provide a regular allowance that would allow Jennifer to live in a style to which she was not accustomed. Perhaps I should have.'' For the first time, her voice betrayed a tremor. ''This might not have happened.'' Eyes cast down, the grand lady became a grieving mother.

Her evident distress induced the stirrings of anxiety in Medeiros, and he waited until she returned her gaze to him before asking, ''Other than his wife, do you know anyone who had a motive to murder your son?''

''No one. Peter sometimes got into silly scrapes, but he only injured himself. He was never mean or ungenerous. He had no enemies.''

''When did you last see or speak with him?''

''I have not seen him since he went to the Cape in early June. He telephoned me about once a week. The last time I spoke with him was Friday night.''

Medeiros's ears perked up. ''When Friday night?''

''About nine o'clock.''

''Did he say where he was?''

''Not exactly, but when I mentioned to him that it was difficult to hear him, he said he was calling from an outdoor telephone and cars were going in and out of the parking lot.''

''Tell me everything he said to you.''

''It was rather garbled. Peter was excited and said several times he was going to make me proud of him. He would atone for all his mistakes. Everything would be settled after a certain meeting that night.''

''Did he give any indication of what it was that he was so excited about or whom he was meeting?''

''No, he was not entirely coherent. I suspect that he may

have been drinking. He also said he wanted to tell Jennifer the good news, but she was not at home.''

''Did he say why he knew she was not at home?''

''Yes, he had telephoned her just before calling me and did not receive an answer. He seemed very eager to speak with someone about his news.''

''Did you have the impression he was referring to the dig on which he was working?''

''He did not specifically mention that, but I assumed he was referring to it. What else could it have been?''

''I don't know, Mrs. Dafoe, but it might be the key to this mystery.''

''Nonsense! It was Jennifer. Why would anyone kill Peter over an archaeological discovery?'' On this point she was intransigent.

Choosing to ignore her recurring accusations of Jennifer, he arose, thanked her for her kindness, and could not resist complimenting her on the decor. The surprise in his voice must have been evident to the astute Victoria Dafoe, because she smiled knowingly and responded, ''What did you expect? An old woman surrounded by antiques and memories? After my husband died that is exactly what you would have found, but Peter convinced me to rid myself of the past. I sold the house, disposed of the furniture, and started phase three of my life. Peter was happier to visit me here than in that old mausoleum. Of course, his relationship with his father was not all it should have been and he was more comfortable away from those surroundings.''

As Medeiros headed for the door, she inquired, ''When will you release Peter to me? I must make the funeral arrangements.''

Nonplussed by this request, he answered hesitantly, ''Since he has a wife, the body will be released to her, Mrs. Dafoe.''

Spots of color appeared on her cheeks. ''That will not

do! I am his mother. You cannot allow a mere interloper to supersede me. She would not know the first thing about a proper funeral. She will probably be in jail anyway.''

Anxious to remove himself from this maelstrom, Medeiros temporized, ''Perhaps Dr. Dafoe's wife would agree to let you arrange the funeral, because, as you stated, she has no expertise in the matter,'' and walked hastily toward the door.

Chapter Eleven

Frank Nadeau had just finished speaking with Dr. Mann, the medical examiner, and obtained preliminary results of the autopsy. Blood, alcohol, and other toxicological tests would be performed at the state police laboratory in Boston and would not be available immediately, but cause and time of death were of more concern to Frank.

Doc Wilson had nailed down both, as the chief had assumed he could. Dr. Mann confirmed death from massive trauma inflicted by a blunt instrument, the injuries consistent with the use of a baseball bat. The lab was matching the blood on the bat and could probably give him a report today. The bump on the back of the head would not have been fatal but might have caused unconsciousness, particularly if the victim was under the influence of alcohol, which appeared to be the case, judging from the stomach contents. Approximately two hours before death, the victim had eaten a meal of clams, potatoes, and an alcoholic beverage whose preliminary analysis was consistent with beer. Without knowing the time of this meal, it was impossible to pinpoint the exact time of death because of the delay in discovering the body, the heat of the day, and the inordinate resident insect population of the shed. Death had probably occurred between nine-thirty and eleven-thirty on Friday night, thirty minutes either way affording a reasonable allowance.

With the prospect of being able to discover the exact time of death as soon as he could interview the staff at The Landing, Frank felt more sanguine about the investigation. But first he had to deal with Jeb Newcomb, who was waiting in the reception room.

Jeb, looking cool and relaxed, was ushered into the chief's office. Deciding to try shock tactics with this cocky fellow, Frank asked brusquely, "Mr. Newcomb, where were you on Friday night between nine P.M. and midnight?"

Expecting an exchange of pleasantries, Jeb was taken aback by the abruptness of the question.

"Friday night! Why are you asking me that?"

"I am asking you because you have been less than truthful with us. You never admitted knowing the deceased, Peter Dafoe," said the chief sternly.

"You never asked me if I did," replied Jeb, his cockiness reasserting itself.

"That is technically correct, I did not. But we did tell Marguerite his name. Do you expect me to believe that you were with Marguerite all day and night and she never discussed the murder or mentioned that name? It would be easy for us to ask her, but I thought you could spare her the trouble and tell us yourself."

"We didn't talk much about the murder because of the boys."

"Okay, let's do it the hard way," said Frank resignedly. "Where were you on Friday night between nine P.M. and midnight?"

"I was at my Aunt Rachel's. Rachel Stowe."

Now it was Frank's turn to be startled. Rachel Stowe, an autocratic octogenarian, was one of the most well-known and least-seen residents of Eastham. Frank reproved himself for not having remembered she was a Newcomb, the daughter of Quincy Newcomb and Faith Howell. Her Cape

Cod connections were prestigious, as she could trace her ancestry through her grandmother, Prudence Beale, back to one of the seven families who founded Eastham in 1644. Rachel's grandfather, Tyler Newcomb, husband of Prudence Beale, served in the Yankee Navy, then became a sea captain and grew wealthy in the China trade. He built a large Greek revival house on the bay in Eastham. Although sea captains usually avoided houses on the water, he was too much of a Yankee to ignore this ten-acre parcel inherited by his wife. Their son, Quincy, started a ship chandler business in Boston with a partner, Silas Stowe. Quincy's daughter, Rachel, married Silas' son, Silas, Jr. Racking his brain, Frank seemed to remember that she had borne two children who died at young ages and had remained childless thereafter. When Quincy died, he left the Eastham house, by then used only as a vacation home, to Rachel, and left his son, Tyler, Rachel's half brother, his share of the chandler business and the house on Beacon Hill. So this must be Tyler Newcomb's son. Interesting! To misquote the late Vince Lombardi of football fame, "Genealogy on Cape Cod isn't everything, it's the only thing."

Collecting his wandering thoughts, Frank asked, "When did you arrive at your aunt's house?"

"At about six o'clock. I had my two sons with me."

"Tell me everything you did Friday night."

"First, I received a tongue-lashing from Aunt Rachel, who likes dinner served promptly at six o'clock. When she settled down we had a glass of sherry and went in to dinner at six-thirty. It was served by Ms. Silva, who acts as a companion, nurse, and general factotum now that Aunt Rachel can't manage by herself. She pretends that she doesn't need the help and is just being kind to Ms. Silva, but that isn't so. After dinner, Aunt Rachel climbed up to the widow's walk on her house and surveyed the sea as she does every day of her life. She has an old rocking chair up there and in mild weather sits awhile before going to her room, where she reads and retires regularly at nine o'clock.''

"Well, that accounts for Aunt Rachel, but what about you?'' asked Frank, making no effort to hide his sarcasm.

"The boys and I went for a walk on the beach. It was low tide and they like to search for shells and hermit crabs. They also like to get away from Aunt Rachel, who believes that children should be seen and not heard. We came in about eight-thirty because it was getting dark. The Red Sox were at Fenway, so the boys and I watched the game. I let them stay up late as a treat and the game was a good one for a change.''

"What time did it end?''

"Late, almost midnight. It went into extra innings. In fact, Jamie fell asleep and I carried him up to bed.''

"Were you in the house all this while?''

"Of course I was, Chief. I was with my sons.''

"Is there anyone who can verify this?''

"Ms. Silva can. She was home and helped me put Jamie to bed.''

"Was she in the room with you watching television?''

"Not all the time. She doesn't like baseball and has a television in her room. She was in and out of the room, though.''

"When did you go to bed?''

"About midnight. As soon as the boys were put to bed.''

With midnight the outer limit for the murder as set by the medical examiner, Frank saw no recourse but to gracefully withdraw.

"Thank you for coming down here, Mr. Newcomb. I am sorry we had to inconvenience you, but we must examine all possibilities in a murder case.''

Expressing neither gratitude for the apology nor acknowledgment of the burden, Jeb arose from his chair slowly and confidently, and, with the merest nod of his head, left the office.

Soundlessly chastised, Frank sank back in his chair, vowing to interview Ms. Silva. He was not so easily put off, even by a Newcomb.

Sergeant Patterson, pulling overtime duty today, reached the cottage at nine A.M.. A phone call had advised the three scientists to remain at home for his visit. They were in various states of dishabille as they sat sleepy-eyed and glum-faced around the formica kitchen table consuming toast and coffee. Since their normal work schedule habituated them to early rising, he concluded that their tiredness was due to sleeplessness rather than the hour.

Refusing an offer of instant coffee, he displayed his search warrant, went directly to Dr. Dafoe's room, and opened the padlock. His instructions had been explicit: search for the missing green notebook and any notes, papers, notebooks, letters, or books possibly pertaining to the mysterious skull.

Patterson worked methodically as befitting a former homicide detective. He removed each drawer from the chest and examined not only the contents but the back and undersides of the drawers and the partition above the drawer. Then he moved the chest itself to check its back panel. Nothing hidden, nothing taped to it. The expected assortment of clothes provided nothing of interest, but a shoe box containing personal papers was removed to be examined more fully at headquarters.

He checked the backs of the mirror and the bed headboard, overturned the mattress, looked at the bottom of the lamp, and used his flashlight to examine the inside of the closet. He ignored the stacks of notebooks on the chest—these were going to headquarters with him—but thoroughly checked the bookcase and shook out each book for hidden papers. Still nothing.

He emptied the laundry bag with no results, then opened the backpack and removed its contents. They appeared to be tools for fine archaeological work: small trowels no bigger than a spoon, brushes of several types, miniature chisels and picks, and a roll of cotton padding. Carefully repacking the bag, he concentrated next on the clothes. Although neatly hung, some of them appeared to have been worn since laundered. Hoping that Peter was as negligent as Patterson himself was about emptying pants pockets, he removed the clothes from the closet and began searching them with immediate results. The back pocket in a pair of shorts contained a neatly folded letter addressed to Dr. Dafoe at a post office box number and dated two days prior to the murder, with the return address indicating it came from a Cambridge laboratory.

Carefully removing the letter, Patterson read that the sample of bone submitted to them had been carbon-14–dated at about 950 to 1,000 years BPE. Sensing the importance of this letter without knowing why it was important, he decided he needed an interpretation of it, and where better to obtain it than in the kitchen? Unhurriedly, he completed his examination of the clothes and returned them to the closet.

"I think I'll take you up on that offer of coffee," he announced, walking back to the kitchen.

Not knowing any casual way to introduce the subject of carbon-14–dating, he asked directly, "If a bone sample has been carbon-14–dated at 950 to 1,000 years BPE, what does that mean?"

Three drooping heads snapped up at this question. George was the first to answer. "BPE means before the present era, which is the same as saying 950 to 1,000 years ago."

"Are you suddenly interested in archaeology, Sergeant?" queried Cynthia.

"Only in so far as it helps us to solve this case," he answered. Swiftly calculating, he remarked, "That would mean the sample was from 993 to 1,043 A.D., wouldn't it?"

"The officer is a mathematical genius," wisecracked Dell.

Ignoring the taunt, Patterson continued, "Could a skull of that age have been taken from your dig?"

"Theoretically, yes, but no skulls have been taken from our dig. We are excavating a home site and not a burial ground. Besides, if you're talking about that skull at the police station, that's not a Native American skull, and there were no Caucasians here that long ago," answered George.

"I guess it started with the Pilgrims in 1620," said Patterson.

"No, before that," replied George, an eager instructor. "The Pilgrims were the first Europeans to settle here, but the French and the British had sailed this and the Canadian coasts for many years, trapping and fishing. Samuel de Champlain named it Cap Blanc in 1605 because of the sand dunes, and he sailed right into Nauset Harbor. He described the Indian houses and the cultivated fields. A few years before that, Captain Bartholomew Gosnold had named it Cape Cod because of the quantity of cod fish, and named Martha's Vineyard after his daughter and the wild grapes growing there.

"If you want to talk about Europeans in the area where I grew up, along the banks of the Hudson River, that was named for Henry Hudson, who sailed north along it in 1609; however, it was first described almost one hundred years earlier in 1524 by Giovanni da Verrazano. He finally got a bridge named after him." George paused for breath.

Overwhelmed by data from this talking encyclopedia, Patterson quickly interjected, "There appears to be a green notebook of Dr. Dafoe's missing. Have any of you seen it since his death?''

In tandem, they shook their heads and answered, "No."

He continued, "It was not in the car and it is not in his room. Since my warrant extends to this entire cottage, I'm going to search the remaining rooms, including the second bedroom. When I'm through, there are certain other items I am going to request of you."

The now fully awakened young people looked at each other and shrugged their shoulders, indicating reluctant acceptance of his authority.

"With the three of us sharing that shoe box of a room, you'll be lucky to find bottom in there, let alone clues." Dell was apparently amused at the prospect.

Their unconcern signaled to the sergeant the unlikelihood of success. People who so readily agreed to a search either had nothing to hide or had already taken care to hide the object elsewhere. Nevertheless, he went through the routine as carefully as he had in Peter's room. The results confirming his original conclusion, he returned to the trio with a question. "There is one thing I don't understand. You are on an archaeological excavation, yet I have searched this whole house and there is not one item from that dig. Where is everything?"

"As you can see, we have no storage or working space here," answered Cynthia. "Anything we remove is first recorded as to exact location, then photographed, and once a week packed and taken back to King's College for further study when we finish here. Since there is no room to work in this cottage, we use the second bedroom in the other cottage. The bed was taken down and folding tables brought in from the college. Any work we have to do is done there, including completing our notes. The camera equipment, our theodolite, and packing materials are there also. The students are learning how to document, describe, draw, and handle specimens. Is there anything else you would like to know?''

''Yes. Would you show me the clothes you were wearing Friday night?''

Eyes widened at the implications of this request.

''Are we suspects, Sergeant? You had better read us our rights.'' Dell again.

''We are only eliminating people right now. Eventually we will eliminate everyone but one and that will be the murderer. As to your rights, they are the same as the ones read to you last night.''

''I wish you would eliminate me right now. I can't sleep well and my stomach is all upset,'' said George.

''Ah, the obvious nervousness of guilt. Arrest him right now,'' joked Dell.

''Just the clothes, please.''

Emerging from the bedroom in a few minutes, they placed an assortment of clothes on the table, dishes pushed to one side. Except for the diminutive size of Cynthia's clothes, the assembled wardrobe was gender neutral. Unisex, thought Patterson disgustedly. In his youth you could tell the girls from the boys. Sorting them out, he was advised that the shorts and tank top were Dell's; the chinos and a faded black T-shirt, George's; smaller chinos and a King's College T-shirt, Cynthia's. After confirming that Cynthia and George had both seen Dell in his outfit and had seen each other in theirs, Patterson examined them carefully. Dell's clothes and the two T-shirts had come out of laundry bags and smelled musty, but had no bloodstains and no signs of having been rinsed to remove stains. The two pairs of chinos had been worn obviously, but were also free of stains and of newly washed areas.

''How about your shoes?''

Sighing, they trooped back to the bedroom and brought

out two pairs of sneakers and a pair of sandals for Cynthia. No blood, lots of sand.

"Just one more point," said Patterson. "Were any of Dr. Dafoe's recent activities different from his usual habits? Did you notice anything strange?"

George answered first. "I never worked with him before, so I don't know if he was acting differently, but he seemed rather secretive."

"In what way?"

"At night he rarely associated with us after the first couple of weeks. He either spent all of his time in his room reading and recording in that notebook or else he went out after dinner and never said where he was going."

"Did he stay out late?"

"Yes, he did," replied Dell. "Strange too, because he never would say where he went. I came in a few nights at the same time as he did, around midnight, and he didn't even hint at where he had been. I figured he had a chick somewhere, so I never asked. He wasn't drinking, though."

"Did you happen to see what he was reading?"

"No," answered George, "but some of them were library books."

"Were they from the Eastham library?"

"I doubt it, Sergeant," said Cynthia. "Peter's interests were mainly archaeological and very technical. Books of that type are not available in the average small-town library. He probably brought them with him from the university library."

"The only trouble with that theory is that there are no library books here now. Where did they go?"

"Perhaps he mailed them back. He left the dig briefly at lunchtime on Friday and said he was going to the post office," suggested Cynthia.

"Good idea. We'll check on that."

Patterson padlocked Peter's room after removing the

shoe box and the filled notebooks, the latter amidst squeals of protest. Assuring them that the notebooks would be returned unharmed, he reopened the room and let each of them take one of the new notebooks from the packages in the closet. Padlocking the room once more, he walked toward the door. Almost as an afterthought he inquired, "Are you working today?"

"No. Dr. Branowski is coming here tomorrow to reorganize the dig. He wants us to meet with him before continuing our work," said Cynthia.

"Prince Valiant to the rescue," added the irrepressible Dell. "By the way, Sergeant, you never did read us our rights again. If you arrest me, I shall go right up to the Supreme Court."

Thinking he would like nothing better than to let this young wise guy cool in a cell for a couple of hours, Patterson merely smiled and departed.

Chapter Twelve

Clam chowder (properly pronounced chowdah) is a serious matter on Cape Cod. Every seafood restaurant worth its salt has a banner proclaiming it the home of the official contest-winning chowder. Home cooks vie for approbation, and in the doughnut shops congregations of retirees while away many gray winter mornings discussing the merits of thick versus thin chowder.

Marguerite had her bucket of quahogs in the refrigerator soaking in water and cornmeal for thirty minutes to rid them of sand. As soon as she showered off the black, odoriferous mud of Salt Pond, she put the clams in a large pot and steamed them briefly to open the shells. Saving the shells for the boys to put on the garden walk, she separated the tough muscles from the soft parts, chopped them finely, and added them to the kettle with well-rendered salt pork, butter, sautéed onions, flour, and strained clam broth. Cube a few potatoes, cover the kettle, and lunch was underway.

With culinary matters well in hand, Marguerite turned to Jeb, sitting under the deck umbrella reading *The Boston Globe* account of the murder. "What did Frank want?"

"Nothing much, Aunt Marge. He was just checking on where everyone was Friday night. He forgot to ask me when he was here."

"Did everything go all right?"

"Of course it did. I was at Aunt Rachel's all night."

She had to admit he did look better. It probably had been a bug bothering him after all. Relieved, she went to the medicine cabinet to locate the cream for his leg rash. It seemed to be worse. He probably had not tended it since yesterday. Her ministrations were interrupted by the telephone.

"Mother, it's Alexandra. What in the world is going on there?"

"Nothing to do with me, Alex. A body was found in our shed. Just a coincidence. How did you find out so soon?"

"The papers. Even in politics-crazed D.C. they feature human interest items from around the country. This one is titled *The Body in the Well Shed* and refers to retired teacher Marguerite Smith, fifty-nine, of Cape Cod and mentions your finding the body of an archaeologist in your well shed. It's just a paragraph—no details. What happened? Are you all right?"

Marguerite answered as fully as she could, hoping to satisfy Alexandra while omitting any references to Jeb. It was not easy. Her daughter was perspicacious and persistent. Question followed answer. Answer hedged the question. Marguerite felt like a naughty child under parental scrutiny.

Self-possessed as a youngster, self-confident as a teenager, Alexandra became self-contained at the age of twenty when she learned her father was leaving them, abandoning wife and children for a younger woman. She never forgave him. Now a professor of English literature and married to Preston Trowbridge of the State Department, Alexandra lived in the Georgetown section of Washington, D.C., in a narrow townhouse as overpriced as it was undersized. Preston's obligatory social engagements suited Alexandra just fine. They provided an opportunity to exercise her linguistic ability and converse with the world's power elite, whom she contrasted, often unfavorably, with her colleagues, the intellectual elite. His frequent government trips were just as agreeable to her, for she was a writer as well as a professor and treasured solitary evenings fueled by a takeout dinner, warmed by a fleecy bathrobe, and stimulated by the beauty of words as she put pencil to paper. Marriage diminished some women. It did Portia, and, to a lesser extent, Marguerite herself. But not Alexandra. She hoarded the best of herself and enhanced the best of Preston to produce a partnership but never a dependency. The betrayal by her father was engraved on her soul.

Parrying question and answer with her formidable daughter, Marguerite finally gained control of the conversation by asking Alex about her writing, her husband, and the weather. Going well, reading the Sunday papers, hot and sticky were the replies. Making her good-bye as brief as motherly affection would allow, Marguerite hung up the phone with relief. She dearly loved Alexandra but did not want her involved in this right now, certainly not until Jeb was gone. Alex had thought her cousin Portia a fool for marrying Jeb, whom she considered a charlatan. That Marguerite tended to agree contrarily made her defense of Jeb stronger.

Time to finish the chowder. Add the chopped soft parts of the clams, milk, cream, salt, and pepper; stir, heat, and set the table on the deck. Then immediately clear the table on the deck and move the lunch settings indoors. The road in front of the house had become a magnet for cars, bicycles, and pedestrians, who had by now read of the murder in the Sunday papers. Otherwise sane adults were taking pictures, children were astride the fence, two preteens on bicycles had boldly ventured into the driveway and were peering down the path to the woods, the yellow tape serving as a signpost. John and James were delighted and basking in the attention afforded to them as insiders. To call the police or not to call the police? Marguerite decided not to decide right now. The chowder was ready.

Twenty-six hours after the discovery of the body of Peter Dafoe, Chief Nadeau and Detective Medeiros were in conference. Vast amounts of information had been accumulated from disparate sources. It was time to assemble the puzzle, identify the missing pieces, and pursue them to complete the picture.

As Medeiros ate his belated lunch of liverwurst on rye, Frank summarized the events at the Eastham end of the trail. Since Jeb's questioning that morning, Frank had spent his time reading the transcripts of the taped interviews as soon as each one came off the word processor (overtime for the secretary), reviewing David Morgan's report of his long conversations with Cynthia, and assessing the material Sergeant Patterson had garnered at the cottage. The chaff was still to be separated from the wheat, but the harvest was promising.

Medeiros, by now finished with his sandwich as well as a small bag of nachos, similarly updated Frank on the results of his search of the Cambridge apartment and the interview with Victoria Dafoe. He then asked Frank if he had a bulletin board and some large paper on which to outline their data. Looking around the station, Frank located an oversize pad on a stand, a visual aid used by the police officer who frequently spoke before school and community groups. Carrying it into his office, along with a box of multicolored marking pens, he set it in a corner and the organizational work began. Two lines were drawn down the length of the large sheet and the resultant three columns were innocuously headed, *Name, Date,* and *Comments.* They pointedly refrained from using the word suspect. The information required several pages and succinctly summarized their case.

NAME	DATA	COMMENTS
1. Jennifer Dafoe	Claims to have been in apartment all night with Jason Moore. Possible motive—money.	Why so indiscreet if hiding affair? Mother claims Peter said Jennifer not home. Insurance? Check Monday.
2. Jason Moore	Alibi same as Jennifer's. Possible motives—money and Jennifer.	Check registry for car. Location of car? Personal finances? Verify gym till 7 P.M.
3. Victoria Dafoe	Not a likely suspect. Hates Jennifer. Would like to blame her.	Claims to have rec'd a call 9 P.M. from Peter. Outdoor phones near The Landing? Deliberately implicating Jennifer?
4. Three students—Joshua, Warren, Donna	Together in Provincetown. No known motive.	Obtain pictures. Send Morgan to P'town tonight to verify Captain Standish.

5. George O'Malley	With Cynthia until 8:45. Alone 8:45–10:30. With Cynthia after that. Motive—professional?	Consider his use of bicycle. Cottage not far from murder scene.
6. Cynthia Williams	With George until 8:45. At Roy's till 10:30. With George after that. Motive—professional?	Did not see Dell at Roy's. Was not seen by Dell. Obtain picture; check with bartender. Are bars out of view of each other?
7. Anthony Della Robbia	At Nautilus from 6:40–9:00. At Roy's 9:05–10:15. At beach 10:25–11:40. Return to Roy's 11:45. Did not enter. Home—12:00 on. Motive—replace Peter at dig and King's Col.	Check Nautilus. Obtain picture. Check bartender at Roy's. Did not see and not seen by Cynthia. Inquire about Rosemary. Check job offer in CA.

| 8. Jebediah Newcomb | At Rachel Stowe's from 6:00 Friday. No known motive. | Verify. Interview Ms. Silva. |
| 9. Marguerite Smith | At Laura Eldredge's from 8:00-10:00. From 10:05 home alone. No known motive. | Verify with Laura Eldredge. |

Frank and Medeiros paused and reviewed the chart. Except for the three students, no one had a good alibi for the critical hours. There was a lot of legwork to be done on those alibis. Of course, most of these people did not have any apparent motive, and both policemen were convinced that this was not a random killing. Running his mind through the myriad of reports he had read that morning, Frank remembered something.

"Al, there is one person we have not listed and have not questioned but who was mentioned by Cynthia and by Jennifer as having a motive—the head of Peter's department at the university. What was his name? Let me check those reports."

Shuffling through the many pages, Frank found it in David Morgan's report. "Here it is, Dr. Branowski. He didn't record a first name. Cynthia claimed he hated Peter and Jennifer Dafoe said the same to me. She also said that she feared Peter because he was smarter and had as good or better connections."

"That's interesting," agreed Medeiros. "And according to Victoria Dafoe, Peter was excited about something that was going to make her proud. Branowski might have had some information about what Peter was doing. If Peter was correct about his supposed discovery, he would have really become a threat to Dr. Branowski's position and might have even replaced him. Just the fear of being replaced might have driven Branowski to murder. He is evidently a very ambitious man."

"I had better add his name to this chart," said Frank as he arose and wrote:

10. Dr. _____? Branowski	Whereabouts on Friday unknown. Possible motive—fear of losing job to P. Dafoe.	Call his home today. Ask him to stop here before going to the dig Monday.

"We had better keep these notebooks out of his hands for the present," said Medeiros, indicating the stack taken from the cottage. "I'll have to give this some thought. They need to be studied by an expert archaeologist for any clues to Peter's discovery. However, I must make sure it is someone who will not use the information for his own purposes. Anything discovered on this expedition is the intellectual property of King's College."

"I doubt if the clue is in those notebooks," offered Frank. "The key seems to be the missing green notebook. Since it was not in the cottage, on the victim, or in his car, it must be in the hands of the murderer."

"We have another loose end that does not fit anywhere on that chart," said Medeiros. "The three people living in the cottage with the victim claim he always locked his bedroom door when he went out. They agree that it was closed on Saturday morning and Dell claims to have tried the knob and found it locked or possibly just stuck. Yet when Officer Morgan entered the cottage, the door was ajar. There were no keys found on the body except for car keys, and no other keys found in his car. The murderer must have wanted something in that room, possibly the notebook, and taken the key. With the cottage empty all day, there was plenty of opportunity to search the room.''

''Good point. We'll have to question the managers. I understand they keep an eye on everything.''

Both men were silent, pondering the complexities facing them. Their concentration was broken by the buzz of the interoffice telephone.

''Chief, I know you didn't want to be disturbed, but Connie Hopkins is on the phone and she said you wanted her to call you as soon as she had that information for you.''

Mrs. Hopkins, the Eastham librarian, had been assiduously tracked down that morning. Phoning her home, Frank had been informed by her son that she was at church and usually went from there to visit her mother. Prying Connie's mother's number from a teenager reluctant to be diverted so long from MTV was difficult, but eventually successful. The located librarian agreed to stop at the library that day and try to identify those book numbers.

''Put her through,'' said Frank. ''Hello, Connie. Have you got something for me?''

''I think so, Frank. First of all, some of those numbers were not from books in our library. Only the ones with an E after them were. The ones with an O are from Orleans but, surprisingly, they also were returned to us in the outdoor book return box. The books from Orleans are sitting on my desk to be delivered back there next week.''

"Hold them, Connie. Don't return them and lock them up. Anything else?"

"Yes, Frank. All the books were on the same topic."

"What was that?" he asked with a curl of anticipation in his voice.

"The Vikings."

Chapter Thirteen

David Morgan had a full agenda that would occupy him well into the evening—and he loved it. Becoming a policeman had been the unenthusiastic choice of an aspiring artist who found his unsold paintings cold comfort for an empty stomach. Good year-round jobs are scarce on the Cape, and the opening for a policeman had answered his immediate, if not long-term, needs. Bright, physically fit, motivated, and, as a plus, an Eastham resident, he was hired, trained, and now led a double life. Equally nocturnal and diurnal, he policed one shift and painted the other, satisfying body and soul. Never had he considered a long-term career in police work—until today.

Yesterday had been a long, exhausting day; he collapsed into bed around midnight after writing his report while memory was fresh, falling asleep instantly and soundly without ever a thought to paint or canvas. Lapsing into a philosophical flight of fancy as he drove to the cottages, he applauded the complementarity of his two vocations and saw himself twenty years hence, in a uniform befitting his exalted rank as a police chief of note, dramatically unveiling his latest artistic chef d'oeuvre to gasps of approbation.

His arrival at Pine View cottage colony startled him and he had to turn sharply into the driveway with tires squealing and dust flying. A boyish grin illuminated his face. He loved to do that.

Before he entered the office, converted to that purpose from a former sitting room, Violet and Ed Barlow were coming toward him from the living quarters. It would have been difficult to get by them even without the squealing tires.

Both sixtyish, he with a hawk nose, sallow skin, and a smoker's cough; she with too-dark hair and too-red cheeks, they both exuded the disillusionment they could not disguise. Their plan to leave the city behind and relax comfortably in the fresh, clean air of Cape Cod had gone awry. Retiring early from their hated factory jobs, they invested their savings in three cottages, newly repackaged as condominiums. Bedazzled by the lure of steady rental income from April to November, then three or four months in Florida financed by their enormous profits, they succumbed to the realtor's rosy picture and bought the cottages in 1986. That and the next year produced respectable but modest incomes. They learned quickly that only July and August were profitable, weather cooperating, and any rentals in the other months merely helped lower the red ink of operating expenses and mortgage. By 1988, the recession was hurting the tourist business and even the summer months did not guarantee full occupancy. Unable to sell and recoup their investment in a depressed real estate market, they grimly held on. With small pensions, and too young for Social Security, they jumped at the chance to become managers of the complex because it provided free housing. It also provided a life of toil, he endlessly repairing the old buildings, she cleaning cottages and doing mountains of laundry, and both manning the office. The winter months brought a respite from work but not from worry, for which they had plenty of time. There were no trips to Florida or anywhere else.

"What can we do for you, Officer?" asked Ed hoarsely. "I guess it's about that murdered fellow."

"Yes, it is. Your house seems to give you a good view of anyone entering or leaving the driveway. Did you see anyone enter or leave going to or coming from Dr. Dafoe's cottage any time yesterday prior to my coming here in late afternoon?"

"You might as well ask me if I saw the moon yesterday. Saturday is a hellish day for us, and we never take a break. The weekly renters check out on Saturday morning and we have to clean up their mess, do the laundry, fix the damage, and get the cottages ready for the crowd checking in Saturday afternoon." His voice was acerbic. "There are twelve cottages here and only two are rented for the season to those scientists. With the weather being so good this month, all the cottages were rented for Saturday. The only cottages I didn't pay any attention to were those two. We just leave clean sheets and towels for them and they do the cleaning themselves. That was part of the deal."

"What time Saturday did you leave them the sheets and towels?"

"No time," answered Violet. "I always leave them on Friday so I can have the soiled ones washed and ready for use by Saturday. Gives me a head start."

"Did you see the occupants of that cottage leave on Saturday morning?"

"Matter of fact, I did," recollected Violet. "I noticed that young fellow with the fancy car coming down the driveway with the other fellow, the one with the glasses. You can't miss him because he drives so fast."

"Did you see the young lady in the cottage leave?"

"Let me think," said Violet, closing her eyes to recall the scene. "Yes, she was getting in her car and had the key in her hand. I kept walking past the cottage to one of the early checkouts, but I heard the car door slam and the motor start."

"Did you see her drive away?"

"I was in the far cottage by then and couldn't see anything," she recalled. "But the car was gone when I came
out a short while later and walked to my house with a load
of laundry. So I guess she drove away."

"How much later did you leave the cottage and walk to
your house?"

"Only a few minutes. Just as long as it took me to strip
two beds and grab the dirty towels. I can do that with my
eyes closed. She drove away, all right."

Thanking them for their help and asking them to call
him if they remembered anything else, he drove down to
the cottages, hoping to find the residents home. Receiving
no answer to his knock, he tried the knob and, to his dismay, found it unlocked despite directions to the contrary.

Maybe they had not gone far. The cottage colony backed
onto a pond, one of its selling features, and occupants made
frequent use of it. David walked down to it and found Cynthia and George lounging in the shade of a tree. The heat
wave had broken and the day was warm but not hot, so he
concluded they were escaping their daily environment of
relentless sun. Dell, alone in the sun, was wearing a closely
fit, minimally sized bathing suit amply displaying the lov-
ing care lavished on his pecs and quads. His tanned, hair-
less body glistened under a coat of suntan oil.

George was clad in a George bathing suit, boxer style
and baggy, insipidly colored, defining the personality rather
than the body. David was surprised at the body, however,
noting the strong, muscular legs and arms whose effect was
neutralized by a stooped posture and lackluster expression.
They had better take George more seriously and check out
that bicycle of his.

Cynthia's look of fragility was exacerbated by her bikini.
This was a woman who looked better covered up, thought
David, whose painter's eye preferred curves to angles. A
movement on a wooden platform in the pond drew his at-

tention, and he noted a young woman preparing to dive. Recognizing her as Donna, he waited until she swam to shore and joined them before he explained his mission.

With four of his six subjects present, he quickly took Polaroid facial pictures of each, with permission readily granted. They seemed to think it a lark and vamped for the camera. David asked Donna the whereabouts of Joshua and Warren, explaining he needed their pictures to help establish their presence at the Captain Standish.

"They are surfing at Coast Guard Beach. But you don't need their pictures, Officer. Just show mine. I was a big hit at karaoke, and those two were loudly encouraging me. The bartender is sure to remember us.

Frank Nadeau sat silently, telephone in hand, his mind groping for an explanation. The librarian thought they had been disconnected. "Frank, are you still there?"

"Barely, Connie. Barely. Were all the books about the Vikings?"

"Every one of them."

"But what do the Vikings have to do with Cape Cod?"

"Some people think they explored it; that Vinland may have actually been in Cape Cod."

"Yeah! Yeah! And my Irish grandmother claimed St. Brendan discovered America. Everyone wants in on it," Frank answered impatiently.

"Every Irish grandmother claims that. And they may be right. The monks on the west coast of Ireland were mystics and were inspired by the desert ascetics of the Middle East. Having no desert in Ireland, they headed for the sea and settled on islands, some only bare rocks, and kept traveling farther and farther. There are traces of monasteries all through the northern islands. When the Norsemen first came to Greenland, they found remnants of stone huts and skin boats, both typical of the Irish monks."

"A skin boat could never cross the Atlantic, Connie."

"Not true, Frank. I recently read a book we have here by Tim Severin that recounts how he planned and executed a trip to trace the sixth-century voyage of St. Brendan as recorded in a ninth-century Latin manuscript. He even had a skin boat built. It's a fascinating book. They eventually succeeded in landing in Newfoundland. Of course, they did not sail straight across the ocean. They took the ancient Stepping-Stone route past the Hebrides, Iceland, Greenland, and then over to the New World. That gave them opportunities to make repairs and obtain supplies. The early northern people were wonderful sailors, Frank."

"Whether my grandmother was right or wrong, I don't know what St. Brendan has to do with my present problem, but thanks for the history lesson. Could you do me one more favor? Since I assume you are leaving there now, could you drop off the books here, even the ones from Orleans?"

"Sure, Frank. I'm on my way. You'll have to pay the fine though," she chided. "Oh, one more thing. I don't know if it is any help, but the books were all placed in the outdoor return box sometime between four P.M. Friday when we closed and ten A.M. Saturday when we opened. Isn't that when your murder occurred?"

Frank whistled at the news. "It certainly was. Are you sure of those times?"

"Absolutely. I emptied the box myself Friday afternoon and the books were in the box when I arrived Saturday just before ten o'clock. I'll be there in a few minutes, Frank."

Patterson poked his head in the door. "I finally reached Dr. Branowski. By the way, his name is Walter, not question mark," he added, pointing to the chart. "Seemed a little huffy at being asked to stop here. He was quick to tell me that the murder was our problem, the continuance of the dig his problem. I suggested, very nicely of course, that we might have to close down the dig. He'll be here,'' Patterson added confidently.

The sergeant was evidently rankled by this Branowski, thought Frank. That seems to be his effect on everyone.

Medeiros studied the house as he walked toward it. Built on a grand scale, it was symmetrically designed with two full stories, white wooden clapboards, and hunter-green shutters. The front entrance featured a portico supported by graceful white columns.

He tapped lightly on the front door. Not that he was intimidated by the possibility of confronting the dowager Rachel Stowe, but because he wished to speak with Ms. Silva privately. Medeiros noted that although Tyler New-comb had flouted tradition by building his house on the beach, he had, nevertheless, positioned it with its back to the sea.

The imposing front door was hesitantly opened by a woman younger than Medeiros expected. Quietly explain-ing his identity and his need to question her, he walked softly into the great entry hall like a trespasser in a shrine. Wealth and power did not awe him, he had seen the dark side of both, but this house was history, his as well as that of the Yankee captains. Medeiros' Portuguese ancestors had served with them on the whalers and the frigates; had endured the same long, hard journeys of three, four, even five years; battled the same storms; survived the same ship-wrecks and shipworms; gaped in wonder at the same exotic sights of faraway lands. What they had not shared were the rewards resplendent before him. No evidence of the ersatz nautical look currently fashionable. No fish nets, or lobster floats, or harpoons, or ship figureheads. These were the tools of the seamen, and displaying them would be akin to a mechanic decorating his home with wrenches and screw-drivers. This home proudly showcased the fruits of man's labors: Chinese vases, Japanese silk screens, hand-painted wall coverings, furniture crafted by the hands of great artisans using precious woods, articles of gold, silver, jade.

Recalling his mission, Medeiros cleared his throat and asked if there was somewhere they could talk without disturbing Mrs. Stowe. Leading him into a small sitting room adjacent to a bedroom, both rooms hers, fashioned from two maids' rooms of a more extravagant era, she bade him be seated and said, "You mean Miss Rachel. She prefers to be called that."

"Do you work here full time, Ms. Silva?"

"Please call me Dolores. My mother is Ms. Silva," she replied with a radiant smile.

He noted that she was dressed in a plain green dress, buttoned down the front, synthetic, resembling a nurse's aide uniform, and wearing stockings, only a memory for most women on a summer's day. Evidently, Miss Rachel had definite ideas how the help should dress.

Answering his question, she continued, "Now I do. I started working here part-time when I was at the community college, but by the time I finished she needed me more often so I came to work full-time and live here."

"Isn't this a little lonely for a young girl like you?" he persisted.

"Yes, but it won't be forever. I get room, board, uniform, and salary, so I live free and am saving my money. When I get enough, I am going to finish college. I need enough money to live off-Cape for those last two years, because there is no four-year college here."

"Tell me about Friday night, the night Jeb and his sons were here."

Dolores recited a narrative much like that already told by Jeb, including the baseball game and helping to put James to bed.

"Were you with Jeb all that time?"

"No, I was in this room. I don't care for baseball and I have my own TV."

"Can you say absolutely that Jeb Newcomb was in this house all night, even say it under oath if we call you to testify?" He was staring fixedly at her as he spoke.

"Yes, he was here all the time. Except when he went out to smoke," she added as an afterthought.

"Tell me about that."

"Miss Rachel does not permit smoking in the house. She does not want smoke to ruin her beautiful things."

"How do you know he went out? Did you see him go?"

"No, I went into the TV room to see if anyone wanted lemonade. I was pouring some for myself. The boys were alone, so I asked where their father was. They said he went out for a cigarette."

"Where did he go for this cigarette?"

"He usually goes out the back door to the beach."

"When did you notice he was gone?"

"It was just before ten o'clock. I was getting ready to watch a show and wanted a drink before it started. I brought in the lemonades for the boys and then went back to my room. I was nervous about leaving them alone, though. If they started wandering into any of the rooms with the antiques, they might cause damage and I'd be blamed. Every time there was a commercial I came out to check them."

"How long was Jeb gone?"

"Until about ten forty-five."

"Are you sure of the time?"

"Yes. When I heard the car coming up the drive I looked at my watch and it was ten forty-five."

Restraining his excitement at this last statement, Madeiros coolly asked, "Did Mr. Newcomb come in the front door?"

"No. He came in the back door."

"You mean he walked all around the house and came in the door from the beach?"

"That's right. It was left open by him, but the front door was locked."

"Does either your room or Miss Rachel's room look out onto the front drive?"

"No. Miss Rachel's is at the back, overlooking the water. Mine is at the side."

"How do you know it was Jeb's car if your room does not look out the front?"

"Because I was walking through the front hall to check on the boys when I heard the car and I went to a window to look out. No one drives up to the house at night so I wanted to see who it was."

"Did Jeb see you?"

"No. The room was dark. I could see him when he got out of the car. He has one of those cars that the headlights stay on for a couple of minutes after you get out."

"What did you do then?"

"I went back to my room and I heard him coming in the back door."

"Tell me about the rest of the night."

"Close to midnight I heard him trying to get the boys to bed. Jamie was sleeping and Johnny was half asleep. I went in and helped him with them."

After ascertaining Jeb's whereabouts on Saturday morning, which were accounted for at all times from when he arose at seven A.M. until he left the house with his sons at about noon, Medeiros moved to end the interview.

"That will be all for now, Dolores. Someone will bring around a statement of what you have told me and you will have to sign it. You may even have to testify to what you said."

Dark eyes widening in horror, Ms. Silva suddenly realized the implications of so heedlessly running her mouth.

Her father always told her she talked too much. But what could she have done? She had only told the truth. Mindful of the castigation forthcoming from Miss Rachel, she asked pleadingly, "Mr. Medeiros, I didn't get Mr. Newcomb in any trouble, did I? Miss Rachel will kill me if I did. He is just like a son to her."

Chapter Fourteen

Chief Nadeau shook out each library book, hoping that a hidden paper would float free and solve the mystery. He did this even though he was almost certain that whomever had returned the books had already done so and the likelihood of his desired miracle was about as great as his getting home on time for dinner tonight. Better call his wife. As he put his hand to the phone, it rang. Answering it himself, he was greeted by Marguerite, inquiring whether he had had any success with the library book numbers.

"As a matter of fact I did. I have a pile of those books in front of me. They are all about the Vikings."

"Vikings! That's a surprise. I was sure they were going to be about Native Americans."

"Why about Native Americans?" he inquired.

"Because that dig of Dr. Dafoe is a Native American dig. And because of that skull. It must have something to do with the murder."

"It probably has, but it is not a Native American skull, it's Caucasian."

"Why would a Caucasian skull interest Dr. Dafoe? The history of the Pilgrim settlers here is well documented. I doubt if he would dig up a cemetery for one of their skulls. That would give him notoriety, not fame. I'm sure it's illegal."

"This skull is not a Pilgrim's. It might be one thousand years old."

Marguerite gasped. "Then we really are talking about the Vikings. That was a time of extensive exploration for them."

"You sound as if you are familiar with them, Marguerite."

"I am somewhat familiar with their explorations, but I'm not an expert and don't have the facts at my fingertips." She paused to think, then continued, "Frank, you don't have time to review those books. Why don't you let me do it? I'm a fast reader; I can scan pages and pick out the pertinent facts. All my years of taking courses under pressure taught me that. You could quickly get a summary of what you need to know."

Frank considered the options. He dearly wanted to know what was in those books that someone had taken such pains to remove from the cottage, and he certainly did not have time to read them. His own staff was spread thinly since the number of temporary summer officers had been drastically reduced by budget cuts and the increased work load of this murder occupied two of his officers. He couldn't use any of the archaeologists on the Viking books because they were too closely involved in this. Maybe an offer from a science teacher should not be refused.

The downside of this solution was her relationship to Jeb Newcomb. But if the answer to this case centered on that skull, it would not involve Jeb Newcomb, because he was not an archaeologist. Perhaps if he had the books examined first, page by page, for anything written on them, and did not let Marguerite take them out of the station, he could use her expertise without risk. Especially since she would not be adding to his overtime budget, which was skyrocketing. Vacillation gave way to pragmatism.

"Okay, Marguerite. Why don't you do that. But since

this is evidence, I can't let you take them out of the station. Can you come here?''

"Sure I can. I'll just take Rusty for a walk first. When am I going to let her loose again?"

"Pretty soon. I'll ask Medeiros if he intends to have those woods examined further. The shed will remain sealed, though. See you in a while."

He forgot to call his wife.

Excited at the prospect of helping to solve the mystery and rid her mind of an albatross, Marguerite took Rusty for a much abbreviated walk, thoroughly cleaned her reading glasses, and collected a supply of pencils, paper, and index cards before leaving.

She hastily scribbled a note for Jeb to read when he and the boys returned from the beach, advising him to help themselves to the hamburgers, hot dogs, macaroni salad, and tomatoes in the refrigerator if she was delayed. She knew he would want an early dinner because they were returning to Boston that evening.

It felt good to have something useful to do.

Data were now forthcoming from the forensic laboratory. The blood on the bat was that of the victim, but the bat had been wiped clean of fingerprints. The piece of paper found by Marguerite was from a three-by-five-inch notepad of a type frequently found in offices and too common to trace. The writing on it was the victim's, having been compared with other written material in his wallet. Fingerprints were mostly smudged, but a couple of them appeared to be the victim's. The others were not clear enough for identification. Frank grunted when he read this.

The dirt and leaves found in the victim's hair were consistent with samples taken from the ground outside the shed. However, this was not conclusive as to origin, because the same types of soil and flora were common to much of the Lower Cape.

The victim's van had no bloodstains but much sand. The driver's seat contained fibers that probably came from the victim's clothes but were a common chino type and identical to fibers found on other seats. Clothes fibers were absent from the floor of the van.

There were at least six sets of fingerprints in the minivan in addition to those of the victim. No other fingerprints had as yet been sent to them for comparison.

The victim had a blood alcohol content of .08, within the legal driving limits in Massachusetts, but he would have been somewhat impaired by alcohol. Stomach content analysis confirmed the medical examiner's preliminary report of fried clams, potatoes, and beer consumed approximately two hours before death. Tests for the presence of other drugs were negative.

The skull in evidence was very old and was to be examined Monday by an anthropologist who would decide whether to submit it for carbon–14 dating to determine its age.

Frank was absorbed in departmental paperwork, on a short sabbatical from the murder case, when Medeiros burst into his office. "Frank, we have to talk."

As he recounted his questioning of Ms. Silva and Jeb's unaccounted-for absence around the time of the murder, Frank shook his head in contemptuous disgust.

"That guy has been playing loose with the truth right from the beginning. The only thing that has been in his favor until now is the apparent lack of motive. He doesn't benefit financially from Dr. Dafoe's death. It can't be because of Jennifer. She told me herself that Jeb gave her up, not vice versa, and that was years ago. It certainly was not professional competition, because their careers are unrelated—an archaeologist and a ship chandler.''

"How about the possibility of a scam?" suggested Medeiros.

"What kind of a scam?" asked Frank.

"Dr. Dafoe had a skull in his possession, Caucasian and possibly one thousand years old if it's the one the lab tested. No known Caucasians were here at that time, but Dr. Dafoe was reading up on the Vikings. Suppose he obtained a skull elsewhere, a European skull that he knew to be old but did not know precisely how old, so he had it carbon-dated. It proved to be one thousand years old, which corresponded with Viking voyages, so he was all excited that night. He had a few beers, then called his mother and maybe his wife. He was going to pretend he found it on the Cape and claim it was a Viking skull. He would be famous.''

"Why would Jeb Newcomb be involved?"

"Peter Dafoe had no money of his own and he could not ask his mother for money for this. She was always ready to rescue him from trouble, but she would not be a party to planning a deliberate fraud. Besides, he probably wanted to impress her too. He needed to set up a dig somewhere other than the site he was working at, where he would bury the skull then discover it in front of witnesses. He would need to hire a team and make it look legitimate. This Newcomb is from a wealthy family, but how is he personally fixed for money? We'll have to look into that, but, in all probability, he could lay his hands on some money. A discovery like that, privately financed, would be very profitable—books, magazines, even a movie. Dr. Dafoe would become a renowned archaeologist and Jeb would make a large return on a relatively small investment,'' conjectured Medeiros.

"Sounds good except for one thing. It seems out of character for Dafoe,'' Frank objected. ''Everyone agrees he was brilliant, but a deliberate underachiever. He could have had a distinguished career but never cared enough about it to try, a bit like a leftover hippie. Why turn to fraud now to achieve the success he never wanted?''

''The magic number, Frank, forty. He was forty years old, not a professor and probably never would be; lived in a studio apartment furnished with his mother's and other people's discards; and, most of all, he was losing Jennifer. They were not divorced, but they might as well have been. She didn't live with him. And this nonsense about her being discreet so he wouldn't know of her affairs—don't believe it. There are always people who love to dish the dirt and cannot wait to tell a husband or a wife the gossip about a spouse. If she is as good-looking as you say she is, she probably has a fistful of enemies, jealous enemies who were delighted to keep Dafoe informed. No question about it; he had lost her and knew it. He needed to do something dramatic to rescue his career. Forty years old, Frank, a dangerous age.''

''You could be right, but it still seems strange that he would involve Jeb Newcomb. If you are right, that would have been the fraud of the century and better kept secret. There must have been some way to shake money from his mother without telling her the truth. The other thing that puzzles me, and has from the beginning, is why in Marguerite's shed? That might have been a logical place to meet if Jeb had been staying there Friday, but he was at Rachel Stowe's house. It is a lot more private there with all that land she has.''

''There are lots of questions to be answered, and only Jeb Newcomb can answer them. Let's get him down here right now,'' declared Medeiros.

''Right. But I'll have to send Marguerite home first to look after those two boys of his. She is going through those

Viking books for me and will give us a summary of the Cape Cod connection. Marguerite's a science teacher, you know, and could be a big help to us," said Frank.

Attempting to keep a note of irritation from his voice, Medeiros suggested, "Could be a big help to her nephew too. Don't let her take anything out of here."

Without a word, Frank rose and left his office in search of Marguerite. He knew that Medeiros' mistrust was logical, if misguided. Al just did not realize what a fine person she was. Nevertheless, the accusation disconcerted Frank and he found himself recalling how many books he had left with her. *Better count them before she leaves.*

Sergeant Patterson was sitting at the bar of The Landing finishing a Diet Coke with a squeeze of lemon. He abhorred diet drinks, but his brawn was in danger of becoming merely bulk. Cutting down on food was too painful a remedy, so he compromised and shunned caloric drinks, confining himself to black coffee and tea, water, and diet sodas. He allowed himself one bourbon and soda at night, a relaxant tested to its limit in his more stressful D.C. days, and an occasional glass of wine at dinner.

The visit had been productive and the Coke was celebratory. The bartender remembered Dr. Dafoe and specifically remembered Friday night. It seems that Dafoe had been in several times before, always sat at the end of the bar, although he drank only seltzer with lime, and ordered his dinner for service at the bar. He was very quiet, did not seem to know anyone. Kept to himself and left after he ate. That is why the bartender remembered Friday night so well.

Dr. Dafoe came in and ordered a beer, drank it quickly, and had a few more. He also ordered dinner and ate at the bar as usual. Even more memorable was the fact that he spoke to the bartender. He seemed excited and repeated several times that this was a big day for him. Told Jim, the bartender, to take a good look at him because he was going to be famous. It would be all settled tonight. Attributing this delusion to the beers, Jim paid no attention to the boasting, just humored him. When Peter ordered another beer, Jim refused to serve him one. Peter took it good-naturedly and said it didn't matter, he wouldn't be patronizing this place anymore. Then he left, making the grandiose gesture of leaving a large tip.

Patterson routinely asked if Jim remembered when Dafoe ate, never expecting an answer from a busy bartender. To his amazement, the answer was within reach. The management was assessing its staff deployment to achieve maximum efficiency and had requested the wait staff to jot the time of food service on the backs of the order slips. Since the bar food orders were relatively few, and the contents of the meal and parameters of time were known, it was a simple matter to locate the order slip. Only one order of fish and chips had been served at the bar between seven-forty, when Peter arrived according to Cynthia and George, and ten P.M., the latest he could have eaten because the medical examiner had set the latest time of death at eleven-thirty, with a thirty-minute leeway, and the victim had eaten two hours previously. Patterson extended his search to ten-thirty for good measure but found no similar orders. The dinner in question had been served at eight-thirty P.M.

Patterson knew from personal experience that the fish and chips dinner included coleslaw. There had been no mention of coleslaw by the medical examiner. Maybe Dr. Dafoe didn't like coleslaw. Perhaps rich kids were not brought up with the admonition to clean one's plate because it was a sin to waste food. Patterson was never guilty of that sin.

Jeb Newcomb strolled into the chief's office with his habitual air of insouciance. Frank appraised his attire, the third outfit he had seen on Jeb in a little more than twenty-four hours. To Frank, a day off meant never having to dress up and wearing the oldest clothes possible, disreputable his wife claimed. Jeb was now outfitted in pleated-front white cotton slacks and a navy blue T-shirt with a collar and the inevitable emblem; only the top siders were a constant.

Jeb was obviously taken aback at seeing Medeiros in the office, sitting to the right of Frank, with an expression of inexorable displeasure. His face cleared of surprise in an instant and he asked casually, "What can I do for you now, Chief?"

"It's what we can do for you that's important," barked Medeiros. "We can throw you in jail right now or we can listen to what you have to say, hopefully the truth this time, and then decide whether to throw you in jail. Read him his rights, Frank."

Astonishment, apprehension, and guile vied for supremacy on Jeb's features. As from a distance he heard a voice droning that he had the right to an attorney. *Not yet,* he thought. *I can still figure a way to get out of this.* Guile won.

"I am asking you once again where you were on Friday night between approximately ten and ten forty-five P.M." Medeiros spoke slowly and distinctly.

"I already told Chief Nadeau I was at my Aunt Rachel's house."

"Tell me this time. And before you compound your problems, be advised that I have a witness who says you were not in the house at that time."

The briefest pause, then, "Oh, you must mean the time I went out for a cigarette. I guess Ms. Silva saw me go out. Aunt Rachel does not allow smoking in her house. You know how these old ladies are," Jeb added, trying to evoke male-to-male comradery and rewarding them with his most charming smile.

"Where did you go for that cigarette?"

"I walked along the beach as I always do."

"Were you on the beach smoking a cigarette until you returned at ten forty-five?"

"It wasn't that long. Ms. Silva must be confused. You know how young girls are about time." The smile was a little forced.

"Yes, I know how old women and young girls are. I have a mother and four daughters, not to mention a wife. I have always noticed how observant they are, particularly about anyone entering or leaving the house. Now are you going to tell us where you went in your car Friday night before ten P.M., returning at ten forty-five P.M., leaving you no alibi for the time of Dr. Dafoe's murder?" Medeiros was newly armed with the information Patterson obtained at The Landing, establishing the time of death at approximately ten-thirty P.M.

Jeb looked away, no longer meeting Medeiros' eyes. He sensed that he was about to be charged with murder. Reality was confronting him, unwinding the strands of his protective cocoon and hurtling him toward disaster.

Turning to Chief Nadeau, whom he considered to be the more empathetic of the two, Jeb dully answered, "I went out to meet Peter Dafoe at his request. We met behind Aunt Marge's well shed. He was alive when I left him. I did not murder him."

Chapter Fifteen

David Morgan had concluded two of his missions with moderate success and was en route to Provincetown for his third and last investigation of the day.

At the Nautilus, they definitely remembered Dell having been there on Friday night. He was not the shrinking-violet type and made no attempt to blend into a crowd. His presence made a statement. The gymnasium manager remembered him executing his intensive workout until sweat oozed from every pore in his body. The lifeguard watched him in the pool, envying swimming strokes superior to his own, and he was sure there were several female observers who would be happy to rush to Dell's defense. Perhaps if the officer came back on Friday night they would be at the pool, because members tended to have regular gym nights. In the restaurant, he was less successful. Yes, Dell frequently patronized it, but no one was positive about which night he had been there recently.

The visit to Roy's also had mixed results. Checking the layout first, David concluded that it was possible for two people to be there on the same night and miss each other if they were at different bars and the place was crowded, a given on a summer Friday. Showing the pictures to the bartender at the smaller bar, he had an immediate affirmation. Yes, Cynthia was there Friday night and he specifically remembered her because she was alone and, he suspected, lonely. Markedly out of place among the bois-terous surfer and pinball crowd, she sat silently nursing a cranberry and Absolut. He spoke to her several times to lessen her isolation and include her in the community of fun seekers. Even his practiced bartender patter elicited only a weak smile and a modicum of conversation. He was not sure what time she left.

David had less success verifying Dell's alibi. One of the bartenders at the larger bar recognized him as an occasional patron but could not say with any certainty whether he had been there Friday night. There had been a second bartender on duty that night but, after completing his shift on Sat-urday, he had asked for his pay and said he was leaving the Cape. No forwarding address. Neither could the bar-tender recall a Rosemary who was there Friday night with a couple of other girls. Who asks names?

Next stop—Provincetown.

David loved the dramatic landscapes of Provincetown in the late afternoon of a summer day. The lowering sun bounced its light off the curvilinear surfaces of the sand dunes in a less aggressive and more conciliatory manner. Pilgrim Lake, by contrast, became dark and mysterious. The barest tendrils of blue mist floated over the bay, visible from the road on this narrow wrist of the Cape.

It was with regret that he turned off the highway onto the claustrophobic thoroughfare of Commercial Street. With a parked car, even a police car, sure to cause a major bottleneck near the Captain Standish, he turned up a side street more amenable to illegal parking. His visit to the bar was brief; the bartender immediately recognized Donna. "She's quite a gal. Had the whole place entertained. I think she can sing too, even without the karaoke. Is she in trou-ble?"

"Not now she isn't," answered David.

"Good. If you see her, tell her to come back here."

David returned quickly to his cruiser to find a Provincetown policeman eyeing it and wrestling with the question of how much courtesy to afford an illegally parked, out-of-town policeman who had not notified them of his presence.

Frank and Medeiros looked at each other with mutual relief. Convinced that Jeb was lying, they had no assurance of their ability to persuade him to admit it. If he maintained his bravura, they had nothing but a man who took an automobile ride at the time of the murder. In effect, nothing at all. But faced with the likelihood of arrest, Jeb's sangfroid shriveled. The immediately inevitable was more feared than a postponed possibility.

Frank unobtrusively slipped out of the room and, with a heavy heart, began the request for a search warrant for Marguerite's house. He was sure that would be the next step. Returning to his office quickly, he found a thunderous silence prevailing. Jeb, head down, looked to be at the end of his tether. Medeiros, in an unexpected gesture of sympathetic patience, was waiting for Jeb to win his battle to fight back tears.

Finally, Medeiros began, "Tell us exactly what happened from the time Dr. Dafoe requested that you meet him until you last saw him Friday night. I would like to remind you that we have read you your rights and that this interview is being recorded."

Jeb did not answer at once. Prudence demanded that he say no more until he consulted an attorney. Pride and avarice warned him that any such move would inevitably involve his family and all would be lost. Tell them only as much as necessary and perhaps they would let him go. "I'll answer the question."

He began. "I had planned to go to Aunt Marge's for the weekend with my two sons, because Portia, that's my wife, was going on a business trip. Friday, shortly after noon,

Peter Dafoe called me and told me he had to see me. I had
not seen him for some time and was never a close friend
of his, just an acquaintance, so I was surprised. I asked him
why he needed to see me and he wouldn't say, only that it
was very important, for my benefit as well as his. I told
him to come to my office the next time he was in Boston,
but he would not hear of that. He sounded frantic and said
it had to be immediately. Since I was going to be on the
Cape for the weekend, I agreed to meet for a drink. He said
no, this had to be a private meeting, no one was to know
of it. I thought he was drunk or drugged, but I humored
him and arranged to meet him on the path to the woods
behind Aunt Marge's house at ten P.M. She plays bridge
on Friday and would not be home yet, so I could just slip
out of the house for a few minutes. He agreed and hung
up.''

Jeb paused. To collect his thoughts or to rearrange facts,
Medeiros wondered, then asked, ''What made you stay at
Miss Rachel's instead of Marguerite's?''

''Shortly after Peter called, I called Aunt Rachel. I frequently call to see how she is, and I wanted to tell her that
I would be on the Cape this weekend and would visit her.
Aunt Rachel is very formal and does not expect people to
just drop in, even me. Ms. Silva answered the phone, and
I asked her how Aunt Rachel's health has been. She told
me my aunt is weaker than she had been just a few months
ago, and increasingly needed help. Then she asked if I was
calling about the meeting with the people from the Conservation Trust. I had not known of any such meeting, but
I knew that for some years they have been trying to convince Aunt Rachel to put her property in trust for them,
retaining her right to live there for her lifetime. Or, failing
that, to will it to them. Her property is contiguous with the
public beach and is the largest private parcel of land along
the bay. There are only a house and a garage on ten acres

of beachfront. Aunt Rachel is elderly and not as sharp as she used to be. She should have representation at meetings, preferably by her lawyer, but she had not called him, according to Ms. Silva. Since the meeting was at nine A.M., I decided to change my plans and stay there overnight to be available for support if Aunt Rachel requested it. So when I spoke with her, I said I would like to come with my two boys and visit her overnight. She likes to see us and readily agreed. Then I called Aunt Marge and changed my plans with her, telling her about my intended visit to Aunt Rachel and that I would arrive at her place about noon Saturday.''

Jeb paused again. ''Could I have a drink of water, please?''

Medeiros, recognizing this as a ploy for time, hated to interrupt the statement, but could not reasonably refuse. Jeb stood up, stretched, walked around a little, and took his time with the water when it arrived. His fear was ebbing, his confidence returning in a mercurial mood swing evident to his questioners. Fearful of losing momentum, Frank gently but firmly took the glass from Jeb and told him to be seated. ''Continue where you left off,'' he commanded.

''Where exactly did I leave off?'' asked the restored Jeb.

Fiddling with the tape recorder, Frank played it back to Jeb's last statement.

''Oh, yes. I cancelled Aunt Marge for Friday night. She was probably glad that I did. We might have delayed her getting to the bridge game with those old biddies.''

Tired of this insufferable young man's egregious comments about women, Medeiros gave him an implacable look and spoke with an exaggeration bordering on hostility. ''Just—tell—us—what—you—did—next.''

Momentarily subdued, Jeb took up the tale. ''After I called Aunt Margie, I remembered my appointment with Peter at her place. I wanted to change it, but I didn't know

where he was living, only that it was on the Cape. On the
chance that he was living in Eastham, where he was working, I called information, but they had no listing for him.
There was nothing to do but to keep the appointment. At
about nine forty-five P.M. I left the house on the pretext of
having a cigarette and drove to Aunt Marge's. I parked in
the school yard and walked across the road. Her car was
gone, so I walked through her driveway and down the path
to the shed.

"Peter was there already. I asked him what he wanted,
and he said he wanted me to stay away from his wife. I
was stunned, as I have not had any relationship with Jennifer for years, not since I was in grad school. In fact, I
never even see her except for the occasions when I meet
both of them by chance. I tried to tell him this, but he
wouldn't listen. He started yelling that he knew I was trying
to steal her from him. About this time I heard a car pull
into the driveway. I asked Peter to be quiet, but he ignored
the request and grabbed my shirt. I tried to push him away
from me, but he lost his balance and fell down. He had
been drinking and it did not take much for him to fall down.
When he did not get right up, I bent down to see what was
wrong and he was unconscious, must have hit his head on
something. Just then Rusty came down the path. I guess
she heard us. She started barking and Aunt Marge called
her, then got a flashlight and shone it toward us. She
couldn't see us because we were behind the shed. I patted
Rusty and she quieted down, but the flashlight stayed on.
Then something attracted her attention, probably a rabbit,
and she ran off into the woods. The flashlight went off.
Aunt Marge kept calling her and she ran out of the woods
and up to the house. As soon as they were both inside, I
checked Peter. He was breathing steadily and seemed to be
more asleep than unconscious. I assumed the beer had
caught up with him; I could smell it.

"I had to get home and did not want to speak with Peter again in those circumstances, but I did not want to leave him there. No telling what kind of animals are around at night. So I grabbed his arms and pulled him into the well shed to let him sleep it off. I closed the door to keep animals out but did not lock it. When I left, he was alive and just had to push open the door to walk away. I didn't want to walk up the path toward the house, because it would have been embarrassing to explain all this to Aunt Marge. I cut through the woods to the far side of her lawn, then went over the fence to the road. That must be where I got this damned poison ivy that has been driving me crazy." As if for emphasis, he paused and scratched his legs. "That's it. That's all I know." He looked at each of them in turn, waiting to be rewarded for good behavior.

Neither officer spoke immediately. Jeb kept looking from one to the other, hoping for a sign of approbation. Finally, Medeiros spoke, voice deceptively soft, expression unyieldingly harsh. "Mr. Newcomb, I guess you think I believe in the tooth fairy too. You just don't get it, do you? You are the prime suspect in a murder. By your own admission, you were with the victim at the time of the murder, quarreled with him, and knocked him unconscious. No one else was there. No one can verify that you left him alive. We have enough right now to get a murder conviction and put you away for life. You were there, all right, but not because of his wife. I actually believe you when you say you were not involved with Jennifer. But, I believe he knew that too. His desire to meet you involved another motive, one he bragged about to two witnesses, a motive you are taking great pains to conceal. You're lying, Mr. Newcomb. Still trying to protect your image even though we are about to throw you in jail. Lock him up, Frank!" Medeiros' voice had gradually risen, decibel by decibel, and the last directive had been shouted. With no further word he walked out of the office, slamming the door.

Silence reigned once again. Jeb, now thoroughly intimidated, was searching the fathomless depths of his being. How much longer could he resist? Damn that Peter Dafoe! It was all his fault. Jeb had not created this situation, had not wanted anything to do with it, and now his life lay in ruins before him. But he didn't want to spend his life in jail, either. Maybe he could still salvage something. Unfortunately, they were not buying the story about Jennifer. Peter must have talked to other people even though he had been insistent about secrecy. Damn, damn, damn him! Jeb had to tell the police more and risk his inheritance. Portia would stand by him. Sure she would.

Frank's patience was rewarded. A defeated Jeb requested, "Chief, ask him to come back. I'll tell you everything. But I did not kill Peter."

Marguerite was totally unnerved. She would have liked to be alone, but she had two restless boys on her hands and she could not shoo them off to the playground as there was still a knot of curiosity seekers hanging about. Food, that was the solution for the boys. Get them at the grill again. Hastily assembling a meal from refrigerator stock, she gave them a choice of hot dog or hamburger and let them cook their own choices. *This weekend will not be remembered for culinary achievement,* she thought wryly, despite her anguish. Poor Portia! And those innocent boys! She felt no need to apologize, even to herself, that her concern for Jeb was belated. After all, he was only an in-law, or out-law, she added derisively.

As Marguerite and the boys settled in the kitchen to eat, the deck still off-limits because of gapers, the phone rang.

Marguerite had begun to hate the telephone but felt compelled to answer it.

"Mother, it's Neil. I read about the murder. Do you need help? Should I fly there?"

Her heart sank. This was becoming a national affair if Neil knew about it in Seattle.

"No, dear. Everything is fine. I am not in any trouble. It had nothing to do with me. I expect it will be solved soon. How is Katie? And little Thomas?"

Why, she thought, *am I into denial with my own children?* Everything is not fine. Neil and Alex don't need my protection any longer. They are adults and capable of handling the fact that their mother is very upset and this murder is touching their family. Nevertheless, she was relieved to have deflected his concern.

"They are both fine. I am hoping to get some breathing space in August so we can fly East to see you. I don't want Thomas to miss knowing the Cape and my side of the family."

"Wonderful, Neil. Come any time. I would love to see you."

A few further exchanges and the conversation ended.

As Marguerite resumed her dinner, she reflected. Alexandra and Cornelius, what fanciful names. They were both selected by her husband, who had resented being plain Joe Smith. Joseph Smith was even worse, with its historic religious connotation. He insisted on impressive names for his children. Marguerite had wanted to name her son Thomas after her own father, but Cornelius he became. Neil, living in Seattle and CEO of an export-import firm, had married a Japanese-American woman, and their son was named Thomas, along with a Japanese middle-name. Marguerite finally had her Thomas, albeit three thousand miles away.

Joe now had what he wanted too. On the return address labels of the Christmas cards he sent his children in the years since the divorce, his name appeared as J. Daniel Smith. Joe had a new name as well as a new wife.

"Everything I told you about Peter calling and asking me to meet him is true. Also about my changing plans and going to Aunt Rachel's on Friday night. I met Peter as scheduled, a little before ten P.M. He was very excited and said he had something wonderful to show me, and he held up a plastic bag. Opening it, he revealed a skull all wrapped in cotton. It scared the heck out of me, because I didn't know why he was showing me a skull. He wrapped it carefully and claimed it was a Viking skull and he had found it on Cape Cod. I asked him what that had to do with me, and he said he had found it on private property and had no permission to dig there. Turned out it was Aunt Rachel's property. He had been studying the theory of the Vikings exploring Cape Cod and was convinced it was correct and that evidence could be found if one looked in the right place. He said it would take too long to explain why he selected Aunt Rachel's property, but I guess it had something to do with being along the beach and never having been disturbed. He said there were other bones that he had left where they were, even the lower part of this skull. He was going to put the skull back where he found it, because the discovery would not be considered legitimate if he removed the bones before they were documented. He only took it out to convince me.

"Peter wanted me to introduce him to Aunt Rachel and help convince her that his theory was well-founded and she should permit him to start a dig on her property without mentioning what he had done. I refused. He became angry and started shouting. I tried to quiet him because I heard a car in the driveway. He grabbed me and I pushed him away. The rest is just as I told you.''

''Tell us again,'' said Medeiros.

Jeb repeated his initial explanation of events from this point.

Frank asked, ''Why did you refuse Peter's request?''

''Because I thought he was crazy. It seemed like some drunken idea of his.''

''But he showed you a skull,'' Frank persisted.

''Archaeologists have lots of skulls. How did I know whose skull that was or where he found it?''

''Did he tell you he had it carbon-dated?''

''I think he did, but it didn't mean much to me. I have heard of carbon dating, but I am not familiar with its use. Besides, I did not believe him.''

''Are you sure you had no other reason for refusing his request?''

''I did have another reason. I didn't want Aunt Rachel to be annoyed by some harebrained scheme. She is not getting any younger, you know.''

''No. She isn't getting any healthier either,'' contributed Medeiros. ''If I am not mistaken, she hasn't been well. Liable to go to sleep one night and not wake up. What would that mean to you, Mr. Newcomb?''

''I would be very sad. Aunt Rachel is dear to me.''

''I'm sure you would cry all the way to the bank. Aren't you her heir?'' Medeiros was guessing.

''How do I know? She does not discuss her affairs with me.''

''Of course not. And you changed all your plans and hotfooted it to her house Friday night to be there when the conservation people came to see her just out of the kindness of your heart.''

''That's right. I don't think she should be taken advantage of and pressured into doing something she might not really want to do.''

''And you especially would not want her pressured into leaving them her property—or should I say your property? That might become a very tempting alteration to her will if the site was discovered to be an archaeological treasure. Imagine how she might react if her property was a Viking camp. She would want it preserved, maybe as a historic park with the family name. Of course, that never occurred to you. You are just thinking of her. She probably has a tidy sum of money too. No children, no brothers or sisters. Only you and your sister. Or doesn't your sister count? You seem to be Miss Rachel's favorite.'' Medeiros had made a few phone calls.

''That had nothing to do with it,'' said Jeb defensively. ''I was only protecting Aunt Rachel's interests. I have my own business and don't need her money.''

''Correction. You used to have your own business. You sold your shares to invest in a real estate scheme that bombed. Now you are only an employee. You have the title of president, but you only receive a salary and have no shares. From what I hear, even that position is not secure,'' said Medeiros.

He was right, Jeb knew. When Quincy Newcomb died, he left his fifty-one percent of the business to his wife, Mary, his daughter, Lucia, and his son, Jeb, with a majority of the shares going to Mary. By dint of their majority holdings, the Newcombs had installed Jeb to succeed his father as president. But it was not a fortuitous decision. Jeb was an inept administrator, bored by details and by the necessity to cultivate the ship owners and quartermasters on whom the business depended. He desperately wanted out and, during the rising real estate market, had sold his shares to his mother and sister, unwisely investing the money with a speculator who had a gifted tongue but little acumen. The money was lost. The Stowe family, with forty-nine percent of the stock, and even his mother and sister, were losing their patience with him. He was sick to death of their pep talks. How he wanted to be free of it all. Aunt Rachel was his ticket on the freedom train. He hoped the train was not leaving without him.

Chapter Sixteen

The chief's labored French had a mesmerizing effect on Marguerite. She listened to the form rather than the substance. Since discovering the body Saturday morning, she had been assuming a remote stance. This had nothing to do with her or her family. Her posture was now untenable as the police arrived with a search warrant. Like the gentleman he was, Frank came in first, alone, to lessen the impact of this legal impertinence. He patiently explained, in French due to the children's presence, the new admissions of Jeb and the necessity to search the house. Putting a positive spin on a negative situation, he assured Marguerite that this could prove beneficial to Jeb if nothing incriminating was located. Pressed by her, he revealed, possibly indiscreetly, that they were particularly interested in a green notebook, a bedroom door key, and blood-stained clothes or shoes. Despite her consternation, she smiled, partly at Frank's efforts to produce words like "incriminating" and "bloodstained" in French and partly at the notion of Jeb doing anything that would get blood on his clothes. Even a nosebleed or a cut on one of the children sent him panic-stricken for Portia—or anyone.

Johnny excitedly asked if this was a bust. Jamie started to cry, Rusty to bark. With the ensuing chaos threatening to overwhelm her, Marguerite decided to abandon ship. Let them look. Let them search. Let them violate her privacy, peer through her possessions, probe her dusty corners. She was too weary to care. Putting a leash on the dog, she left the house with Jamie holding her free hand and Johnny reluctantly holding Jamie's hand. She walked purposefully down the driveway and onto the road, averting her eyes from the obtrusive police car and intrusive voyeurs.

Police headquarters had a palpable air of tension. A serious decision had to be made. Should Jeb be arrested or released? At the very least he could be held for withholding information. But what about the murder? Was he the one? There was certainly enough evidence to present to the district attorney. Jeb was on the scene at or near the time of the murder and, by his own admission, had left the victim unconscious. And he had a motive.

Or did he? That was one of the troubling factors. Rachel Stowe had gradually become a recluse. Each year she appeared in public less and less until now she was rarely seen at all. Her doctor, an old friend, came to her home—the only house call he made. Once every six months, Seth Hall, general factotum to Rachel, came with his hired car and drove her to Boston for a dental visit and any business she could not conduct by mail. All other affairs were handled by correspondence or through her lawyer. She rarely had visitors and spent most of her day in her huge bedroom, which extended across the width of the house facing the bay.

Frank had seen this room years ago while investigating what Miss Rachel had claimed was an attempted burglary, despite no evidence of one. Designed as a private sanctuary for parents to occasionally escape a house full of children, one side of the room, as large as a sitting room, was outfitted with a second fireplace, two easy chairs, a chaise longue, a desk, a small round table with chairs for afternoon tea or evening cocoa, and several bookcases. She descended the stairs three times a day for meals in her formal Chinese dining room. Each descent was followed by an inspection of every room on the ground floor.

Her isolation from casual human contact made her increasingly suspicious of anyone who sought her out. She had a reputation among shopkeepers as cantankerous, for although they had not seen her in years—their goods were delivered to the house or picked up by Ms. Silva—she routinely contested their bills. She was tolerated by them with forgiving affection, for she was a link to Cape Cod's nautical history of free-spirited adventure.

Frank drew this verbal portrait of Miss Rachel to clarify for Medeiros his uncertainty as to a motive for Jeb. It seemed to Frank that Jeb would have just had to say no to Peter and the possibility of a dig would be precluded. Any attempt on the part of Peter Dafoe to approach this suspicious and irritable woman would have been ignored or rejected. If Jeb became aware of such an effort, and he would, it was an easy matter to discredit Peter as a bounder with his history of drinking, drugs, and general failure. Even with Jeb's introduction and endorsement, approval was unlikely to be forthcoming. The motive was tempting but chimerical.

Medeiros found Frank's doubts mirroring his own. Jeb was mendacious and avaricious, but he seemed to be more inclined to temporize and improvise than to respond in such an immoderate, passionate, and bloody manner. Especially when the situation lent itself to procrastination or even outright refusal.

There was another matter troubling Medeiros. Ms. Silva had accounted for all of Jeb's time on Saturday morning between seven A.M. and noon, and he was with Marguerite from shortly after noon to about three-thirty or four, when she left for the beach. The murderer had evidently taken Peter's bedroom key from his pocket and searched his room in the cottage, removing the green notebook and, possibly, the library books in order to eliminate any clues to Peter's discovery. The books might have been returned by Peter himself on Friday evening, but he was unlikely to have put the Orleans books in the Eastham box. The bedroom could only have been searched during the early-morning hours by one of the three people living there, or by another person who waited until the trio left for the dig at shortly before eight A.M. Jeb could not have reached there until at least four P.M. and that was too late to search, because he knew the police would be there or arriving soon. That would also compound the mystery of the library books, because they were returned before ten A.M. on Saturday. Although the door to Peter's room was closed in the morning, no one verified whether or not it was locked. Dell claimed he did not pull it hard. David Morgan found it ajar, but that was not definitive. Dell's trying it in the morning might have loosened it so that it opened spontaneously sometime after the team had left for the dig, possibly even with the motion caused by the front door closing or opening.

Both officers considered the green notebook important. Its disappearance magnified its significance. With the lack of any corroborating evidence and without an uncontestable motive, all they had was someone who had quarreled with Peter around the time of the murder. Jeb would have the best defense lawyer available. They needed more evidence. Especially since there were several other people with more cogent motives: Jennifer and/or Jason for money; Dell and Dr. Branowski for professional advancement and security, respectively; and Cynthia and George, who had no clear motives at this point, but they were living in the cottage and had to be considered.

"Frank, we are up against Occam's razor," concluded Medeiros philosophically.

Frank raised his eyebrows.

Medeiros explained. "That's a scientific theory that my daughter spouts at me whenever she thinks I'm asking too many questions. It states that the simplest of competing theories is preferred to the more complex. I find it works pretty well in police investigations too. But this is one of those cases where we might find it more advantageous to ignore that razor, at least temporarily, and release the suspect who was at the scene of the crime."

"Maybe we can follow Murphy's Law instead, and prove that anything that can go wrong will."

Marguerite awoke early on Monday. To be more precise, she arose from bed early. She never really slept at all. Shortly after the police completed their search of her home, Jeb returned, a humbler, shrunken Jeb, still shaken from his experience. Marguerite's reaction to this altered persona was intriguingly paradoxical. She had predicted that Portia would come to grief with this marriage, having seen through the smooth facade and noted the wrinkles of character. Presented with the opportunity to gloat over her prescience, she rejected this unsavory emotion and grasped at the concept that individual fallibility is not synonymous with murderous instincts. Jeb was innocent. He was being singled out by the police because his privileged background made him unlikely to evoke public sympathy. How dare they!

With Jeb exonerated by her jury of one, she was determined to uncover the real motive for the murder. Convinced it had something to do with the Viking theory and that mysterious skull, something other than Jeb's quarrel with Peter, she turned to her notes as soon as Jeb and the boys left for home. Likely to be denied further access to the books at police headquarters, she reread what she had garnered thus far and turned then to her own extensive library for additional information. Failing to complete the picture to her satisfaction, she decided to visit the Eastham library and others, if necessary, first thing in the morning to locate the missing links among this labyrinth of information.

Nervous anticipation had kept her from sleeping and now, at seven A.M., she was walking Rusty. Since the library did not open until ten A.M., she vowed to give her garden some attention. The gloriosa and gladioli needed staking; the coreopsis, daylilies, and balloon flowers were begging for dead heading; and all of the flowers needed to be reassured of her continued appreciation of them despite her recently flagging consideration.

Police stations never sleep; they sometimes nap. Monday mornings were not such a time. The weekend rush of business begat a myriad of details and a mountain of paperwork. Add a murder to the sum, and order was achieved only by the assiduous discipline of Chief Nadeau. Reaching his office at seven A.M., he spent two hours sorting through every police call of the weekend, assuring himself that the citizens and visitors of Eastham were being properly served by its police department. Only then did he turn to the matter of Peter Dafoe.

Phone calls were the first order of business. Medeiros and Frank divided the calls between them and learned the answers to many of the questions unresolved on their data sheet.

The insurance company named on the receipt from Peter's Cambridge studio had a policy on Peter Dafoe's life with Jennifer Dafoe as beneficiary. The amount? Half a million dollars. The manager was advised that Dr. Dafoe's death was due to murder, perpetrator unknown. Forewarned, the manager made a note on the file that the claim was not to be paid until further notice.

Jason Moore had a car registered to him, a 1993 Volkswagen Cabriolet, dark green.

The lab in Cambridge confirmed having performed carbon-14 dating on a specimen of bone submitted to them by Dr. Dàfoe, the source of bone unknown to them. Yes, they had just received a skull delivered by the state police and would date a sample of that skull.

A call to the personnel officer of Stamler University, California, where Dell claimed to have been offered a position, reached only the answering machine. Frank had forgotten the time difference. He left a message requesting a return call.

It appeared that J and J needed further investigation. Motive had been established. Jason had a car, its whereabouts as yet unaccounted for on Friday night. Their alibi was full of holes. They supposedly had spent the night in Jennifer's apartment, in itself suspicious, yet they were not there at about nine P.M. when Peter called. Another trip to Boston was a priority today.

First they had to deal with a minor media frenzy. This case had attracted the attention of journalists bored with murders involving crack dealers or domestic violence. The public was surfeited with the routineness of these stories. A murder involving a body found in the well shed of a retired teacher in a picturesque Cape Cod community was news. The victim was an archaeologist, no less, with a beautiful wife and a prominent mother. Add the questioning of a scion from an eminent family and the claim of a Viking skull (Frank was furious at these leaks), and the media were frothing at their collective mouths. The story no longer confined to Cape Cod reporters, representatives from Boston and all of New England, even from New York, were barreling down Route Six and, like homing pigeons, alighting outside police headquarters and Marguerite's house.

Medeiros, accustomed to the necessity of keeping the

media informed without informing them of anything, had agreed to meet the press at nine-thirty A.M. on the lawn in front of the station. He and Frank collaborated on a brief statement couched in the jargon police never use among themselves but which the media and public have come to expect. They were following up on many leads, had information that could not be released at present, had made no arrests, would not comment on any suspects, were working closely with the Eastham police, would certainly keep them informed of all developments. Taking no questions and agreeing to meet them the next morning, same time, Medeiros, with Frank beside him, turned and walked back into the station, leaving the reporters to invent ways of turning this noninformation into an exciting story. They would resort to that vintage technique called "background": pictures of the dig at the beach, Marguerite's house (the murder scene), and the two cottages; interviews with local people who, in July, would be mostly tourists; and, lastly, as many filler lines as needed with the history of Eastham obtained from a beleaguered librarian.

"Chief, I have a telephone call on hold for you. It's from an insurance company. The woman says it's important and would wait." The dispatcher was besieged with telephone calls, few of them the normal emergencies. She hoped no one seriously in need of assistance was trying to reach them this morning.

"Good morning. This is Frank Nadeau speaking."

"My name is Anne Wells, from New England Insurance. I spoke with you earlier concerning the life insurance policy on Peter Dafoe. The beneficiary, Jennifer Dafoe, was in here soon after our conversation making a claim. The clerk who handled it was new and when he looked at the file, he told her it was a murder and we would not pay. This is not the way it should have been handled, but the damage was done. Mrs. Dafoe became enraged and threatened to sue us. I intervened and told her I was sure she would be paid; this was only a formality and, in any case, she needed to present a death certificate. I am calling to inquire if you have any new information for us and if you expect this case to be solved soon. We are in a difficult situation,'' she concluded anxiously.

"We hope to solve it soon, but we cannot give you anything definite at this time. What we can do is hold up the paperwork on the death certificate. That will buy you a couple of days' time and, who knows, it may be over by then.''

"Thank you, Chief Nadeau. Please keep us informed. We do not want to find ourselves in a lawsuit.''

Frank had barely repeated the conversation to Medeiros when the intercom buzzed. "A Dr. Branowski to see Detective Medeiros.''

Medeiros had never met the chairman of an archaeology department, but did not expect what he saw, particularly after meeting the group in Eastham who, in appearance, resembled beachcombers more than scientists. Walter Branowski was not molded in the robust Slavic image but was a delicate, Chopinesque figure. Slender, of less than medium height, fair-skinned, with fine dark hair falling obstinately over his forehead, handsomeness foiled by his whimsical suggestion of a chin, he extended a soft, manicured hand and introduced himself as Dr. Branowski.

Speaking in a beautifully modulated voice with a regionless upper-class accent, Dr. Branowski informed them that he was a very busy man, especially because he now had the personal responsibility for the Coast Guard Beach dig, but he understood his civic duty to cooperate with the police and was delighted to do so providing they did not take too much of his valuable time, particularly since this regrettable misfortune obviously had nothing to do with him or with King's College. All in one smooth breath.

Recognizing the need to seize the initiative, Medeiros countered Dr. Branowski's pomposity with bluntness.

"You are wrong, Dr. Branowski. This murder has much to do with King's College. The victim was one of your staff, on an archaeological dig under your auspices, and in the possession of an apparently ancient skull that may have been the reason for this murder."

Unruffled by this suggestion, Dr. Branowski slightly adjusted the trousers of his blue-and-white corded suit, carefully avoiding wrinkles, and checked the knot of his tie, pulling it even closer to the collar of his immaculate white shirt, standing firmly starched even in the warmth of a July day.

"Nonsense! Peter Dafoe was a known drunk and drug addict. His past caught up with him. He was probably murdered in a drug deal."

"The autopsy revealed he was clear of drugs," said Medeiros.

"For the moment. He was probably trying to buy some to start again or even to sell some for money," observed Dr. Branowski.

"That still would not explain the presence of the skull. Dr. Dafoe claimed it was a Viking skull found on Cape Cod."

"Absurd! Absolutely absurd!" Color began to rise in Dr. Branowski's hitherto pale face. "The Vikings never traveled farther south than Newfoundland. I have personally led excavations confirming Newfoundland as Vinland and have written extensively on this subject. I am an authority on Vinland." He drew himself a little higher in his chair. "There have been archaeologists, even at King's College, who have tried to gain attention for themselves by claiming the Vikings traveled farther south. I have read their pseudoscientific articles full of fantastic suppositions and wild inexactitudes. They are false, all of them. Lies! I will not

stand for a member of my department spouting this gar-
bage!'' Face fully red now, voice raised almost to a shout.

Whatever happened to academic freedom? thought
Frank.

''We must examine this murder from all angles, professional as well as personal. It would not be the first time
murder was committed for reasons of professional jealousy.'' Medeiros rubbed a little salt into the wound.

''Jealous? Of Peter Dafoe? No one in his right mind was
jealous of Peter Dafoe,'' commented Dr. Branowski
calmly, trying to recoup his image. ''No, Officer, I suggest
you look for another motive for this deplorable act. One of
your usual criminal types, no doubt.'' Condescending now,
and glancing at his watch. ''I must depart. The team is
waiting for guidance from me. Of course, I shall assume
direct control of this expedition myself and shall place Mr.
Della Robbia in charge of day-to-day operations, reporting
to me at every step. Fine family that boy is from, you know.
My obligations do not permit me to remain here to personally supervise the dig, I regret to say.''

I bet you do, thought Medeiros. Hot sun, sand in your
shoes, broken fingernails, living in a cramped cottage—not
quite your style.

''Now, if you will return to me the notebooks I understand you took from the cottage, I shall be on my way,''
Branowski announced, standing dismissively as he spoke
and buttoning his jacket.

''I am afraid we cannot do that,'' said Medeiros with no
sign of regret. ''They have already been sent to Dr. Con-
stantine Athanostos. He is assisting us.''

Purple was now the shade of Dr. Branowski's face.
''How dare you? They are the property of King's College.''

''Yes, they are,'' agreed Medeiros, ''and they will be
returned to you unharmed. They also may contain a clue
to this mystery, but we needed someone to search that out

for us, someone who would understand the notes in them. You will agree, I am sure, that Dr. Athanostos has impeccable credentials and is of unquestionable honesty. In addition, he is retired and has no interest in further explorations or discoveries on his own behalf. His chief interest now is hybridizing and developing new strains of irises. Your notebooks are safe with him.''

''I shall take this up with your superiors. Those notebooks must be returned immediately.'' With that he turned and walked toward the door.

''One more question before you leave, Dr. Branowski. Can you tell us where you were on Friday night at about ten-thirty P.M.?''

Chapter Seventeen

"Mr. Santangelo, thank you for returning my call so promptly," said Medeiros to the personnel director at Stamler University. Briefly, he explained that they were doing background checks in an investigation, just routine, and needed some information on Anthony Della Robbia.

"You must be referring to that murdered archaeologist. Was Anthony working with him?"

My, how this news has spread. "Yes, he was a member of the team. We are checking all their backgrounds. Normal police routine. I would particularly like to know if Mr. Della Robbia had a teaching position waiting for him at your university."

"Normally, I would not be the one to answer that question. Although I am in charge of the personnel office, my hiring decisions are confined to support staff and, of course, we do all the paperwork for academic staff. Their hiring is much more complicated and involves the department heads, deans, the president, and, sometimes, the board of trustees. This is one decision I can tell you about, though, because I was involved. Have you ever heard of the Della Robbia family?"

"No, I can't say I have except for the young man working here," answered Medeiros.

"I can tell you have never been to San Francisco."

"You're right. I haven't."

"The Della Robbias are as well-known in San Francisco as the Pilgrims are in Cape Cod. They have the largest restaurant on Fisherman's Wharf and smaller, tonier places in nearly all of the other districts. About the only place they do not have a restaurant is Chinatown. However, the restaurants are only the tip of the iceberg. Their wholesale fish business is the largest in California, maybe in the United States. They ship all over the world, even send some of our West Coast fish to you in Cape Cod. The business is called Pacific Enterprises. It was started by Anthony's grandfather, also an Anthony, who sold boiled shrimp and squid salad by the cup from a little stand on the wharf. He eventually opened the restaurant and the rest is history.

"His son, Dominic, had a real knack for business, and kept expanding. Didn't forget his roots though. He still lives in North Beach in the same house in which he was born. His widowed mother, Angela, lives downstairs. Gossip has it that Dominic's wife, Julia, from the more genteel Pacific Heights district, dislikes North Beach and has always wanted to move. Evidently, Dominic promised her that they would move, but not while his mother was alive. Angela Della Robbia is as strong as an ox, so that is not likely to be sometime soon. Julia got her way on college though; insisted her son go east to an Ivy League school. Young Anthony is evidently very bright and had great marks, so that was no problem."

Medeiros grimaced through much of this elongated family history and interrupted before more tidbits would be forthcoming. "What about the job offer?"

"Oh, yes. I was coming to that. As I told you," he continued a little petulantly, "Dominic did not forget his roots and belongs to the Sons of Italy. My father still lives in the old neighborhood and knows Dominic from way back. At one of their dinners, over a year ago, Dominic asked my father if I was still personnel director here. When my father said I was, Dominic asked him for a favor. It seems he had done my father a service years ago when Pop was having trouble getting a license for a barbershop. The forms were too complicated for his limited English. Dominic arranged for Pop to meet with his lawyer, at no charge to my father, and the license was soon obtained. Now he wanted a job for his son, in California. He was afraid the boy was going to stay in the East and they would lose him. Dominic is old-fashioned in that way. The family has to stay together. He was hoping Anthony would take an interest in the business and succeed him. My father promised he would ask me and I checked with the head of the archaeology department. By happenstance, they anticipated an opening in September, but were skeptical when I mentioned a Della Robbia. They assumed he was just a spoiled rich kid and wanted to check his credentials before confirming the opening.

"Evidently, they were pleased with what they discovered and agreed to interview him. I phoned and asked him to come for an interview with employment as an object. He flew out here, met the department head and the dean, who were both very impressed with him. His hiring was all but assured, just some formalities that needed completion. He accepted, then dropped a bomb. He was not interested in starting to teach in September, because he was committed to a couple of digs for that year. Please hold the job for him until the following year. The sheer effrontery of it appalled them. One of the most prestigious universities in the country was offering him a position that people would die for and he was arrogantly expecting them to hold it open for a year. Needless to say, that was the last of Mr. Della Robbia. The position was filled by an extremely competent young woman." Mr. Santangelo bristled at the recollection.

Medeiros had been shifting the phone from ear to ear

and was relieved to thank him, agree that, yes, Mr. Santangelo probably would enjoy a visit to Provincetown, and say good-bye.

She just missed looking demure. The simple beige linen shirtwaist dress was befitting a grieving widow, but Jennifer had pulled the wide belt a little too tightly, the better to emphasize her assets. Matching beige linenlike shoes were too high-heeled and pointy-toed. The blonde mane was tamed now in a schoolgirlish ponytail, brashly held in place by a large red bow. Makeup was judiciously minimized, accenting even further the brush of false eyelashes. No jewelry except for her wedding ring, an elaborately engraved gold band that appeared to be an antique, possibly a Dafoe family heirloom.

Frank thought she looked more beautiful than during his initial meeting with her, but also more vulnerable, like an actress playing a role without a script.

It was shortly after eleven A.M. when J and J had arrived in Eastham, wasting no time after their earlier unsatisfactory visit to New England Insurance. Jason was a most attentive escort, holding Jennifer's arm, guiding her to a chair, and solicitously hovering about. He too was clad in beige linen (did they shop together?) but his trousers had no error of taste. Impeccably tailored with that loose-pleated front that makes slim men look slimmer and fat men fatter, they were accompanied by a discreet navy-blue shirt, silk of course. Simple brown loafers and tan socks completed his attire, a look at once restrained and elegant.

While Medeiros was taking the measure of the two visitors, Frank once again expressed his sympathy to Mrs. Dafoe. Unsure of her reason for this visit but suspicious that it was somehow connected with the insurance company, he waited for her to take the initiative. Clearing her throat, fidgeting in her seat, opening and closing a tacky red leather pocketbook, she seemed in no hurry to do so. With barely concealed impatience, Jason prompted her. "Jennifer, why don't you explain why you decided to come here today to assist the police?"

"Yes, I, er . . . I have something to give you." Delving into the pocketbook, she produced a small tape. "This is the tape from my answering machine. There is a message from Peter on it. We thought it might help you find the murderer." Her slender hand, nails unnervingly red, extended the tape toward Frank as if bestowing an award.

Medeiros entered the dialogue. "When was this message left on your answering machine?"

"Friday night. Peter says on the tape that it was nine o'clock."

"According to your statement, you were in your apartment all night. Why didn't you answer the telephone?"

Jennifer looked toward Jason, hoping for rescue. Jason declined to intervene, sensing that Jennifer was more likely than he to receive sympathetic treatment.

"Because I wasn't there at nine o'clock. I was upstairs in Jason's apartment."

"So you lied to Chief Nadeau about your whereabouts on Friday night," Medeiros persisted.

"No, I was confused because I was very upset. Remember, he had just told me my husband had been murdered. When he asked me where I had been Friday night, I automatically said I was at home. I really meant I was in that house, but not necessarily in my apartment. When I later realized you thought I meant my own apartment, I didn't correct you because I was afraid you would think I was changing my story," she concluded, shifting her focus to Frank. Tears were welling in her eyes and tangible fear was evidenced in her face. Urged by Jason, Jennifer had launched a balloon and was not certain where it had landed.

Frank recalled that Jason had confirmed Jennifer's statement that she had been in her apartment. Was he also confused and upset, or was he giving himself an alibi?

"What has happened to make you come forward now?" asked Medeiros.

"I listened again to the tape. Peter claims he was meeting someone. That must have been the person who murdered him. Someone else had a motive. It wasn't me," she added frantically.

Well, what do you know, thought Medeiros. *The talkative insurance clerk who told Jennifer they could not pay because it was a murder had inadvertently stirred the pot. Jennifer is frightened and trying to convince us of a motive other than hers.*

"You have not been charged with anything yet," declared Medeiros, "but you have lied and you have withheld evidence. If there is anything else about which you have misled us or if there is any other evidence of which you are aware, you had better speak right now. The truth this time," he emphasized.

With a faint smile, she tried to assure Medeiros of her veracity and cooperation. Everything was exactly as she had told the chief, except that they had been in Jason's apartment until a little after nine. When she played back the message, she did not think it important. Not until after Frank's visit did its implications occur to her, and by then she was too confused and upset to tell them. Jason had convinced her to come forward and she was very grateful he had, because she had nothing to hide and felt the better for it. She reached over and squeezed Jason's hand.

After locating an answering machine on which to replay the message, Frank and Medeiros heard Peter's voice for the first time.

"Jenny, it's Peter. It's about nine o'clock Friday night. Where are you? I have something important to tell you. I have made a stupendous discovery and will be famous.

Everything is going to be better with us, honey. You'll be proud of me and we'll be together again all the time. I have to meet someone tonight to take care of the details. I'll call you again tomorrow with more information. Love you, Jenny. 'Bye.''

There was a respectful silence of mourning for a man so full of expectations at nine P.M., who lay dead in a well shed less than two hours later.

The remaining six members of the archaeological team plodded about the dig in a desultory manner. Sleepless at night, bedeviled by police during the day, and now, the final insult. That supercilious popinjay, Dr. Branowski, had advised them that since no one on the team had the requisite ability or experience to manage this dig, he would assume its leadership (and credit, no doubt). He had probably gotten word that some of the material they had sent back to the college from the dig might be the oldest Native American artifacts discovered on Cape Cod.

Accompanying them to the beach for his first inspection tour, he went no farther than the pavement closest to the dig, peered out to the site, then advised them that Mr. Della Robbia would assume charge of the petty details of actually digging, while he, Branowski, would shoulder the intellectual burden of interpreting their results and preparing the final manuscript. With that pronouncement, he walked back to his BMW, distastefully wiped sand from the soles of his handmade shoes, and departed without a glance in their direction.

Medeiros was on the phone with the state police detachment in Boston requesting assistance with matters relating to Jason Moore, specifically, verification of his time at the gym on Friday night, the whereabouts of his car on the same night (the name of his garage having been obtained before he left police headquarters), an assessment of his financial status, and a check with his two employers, artistic and culinary, when Marguerite bustled in looking like the Welcome Wagon. She bore a platter of fresh turkey-breast sandwiches, the small breast having been roasted while she gardened that morning, topped with homemade cranberry relish, the last of the previous year's crop from her freezer. Desperately wanting to talk with them, but unsure of her welcome since Jeb's debacle, she had resorted to her old ally, food. If she could keep their mouths full long enough, she could tell them what she wanted them to know.

Marguerite wasted no time. "Frank, I have been reading about the Vikings. Dr. Dafoe's claim of finding Viking remains could be legitimate. If he was correct, he would have made the greatest archaeological discovery in North America. He would have been as famous as Heinrich Schliemann, the discoverer of ancient Troy. But Dr. Dafoe's secrecy made him a murder target. Someone could have stolen his discovery with impunity. This is one of the strongest motives for murder you will ever encounter. The person would be assured of wealth and position as well as a place in history. While you are eating, let me tell you why Dr. Dafoe might have been right."

She reached into her purse and extracted a quantity of three-by-five-inch lined index cards. Feeling pressured by the urgency of time and the number of cards, Frank started to protest, "But, Marguerite—"

"Shh, Frank. Don't talk while you are eating. Or get excited either. It can upset your ulcer."

"I don't have an ulcer," he objected.

"You will if you don't relax a little and have a proper lunch," she admonished. Index cards in hand, she started her lesson, brooking no interference from unruly police officers.

"As any researcher does, I would like to establish my

sources. The books I used relied principally on the *Flate-yjarbók*, which means Flat Island Book. It is a narration in Old Icelandic written between 1385 and 1388 and is in a parchment folio in the *Corpus Codicum Islandicorum,* written by two Danish priests and given to the King of Denmark in 1647. They probably copied it from manuscripts in a Benedictine monastery in Ireland. This was not unusual, because Irish monasteries had long been a repository for intellectual treasures from scholars fleeing upheaval in other parts of Europe. There is an even older book, the *Landnámabók* from twelfth-century Iceland, describing how the Norsemen reached Iceland from Scandinavia and found Irish priests living there. But that is another story.''

Frank and Medeiros looked at each other, rolling their eyes in relief at being spared another St. Brendan story. Ignoring their silent commentary, Marguerite continued.

''The Vikings were superb seamen and took long voyages. They sailed southward to Sicily and eastward, then down the whole length of the Volga. They were known and feared throughout coastal and river-accessible areas of Europe, because they were aggressive and fierce. That is where our story starts.

''About 970 A.D., Thorvald of Norway committed manslaughter and was exiled. He went to Iceland with his red-headed son, Eric. Finding the best land already taken, Eric married and moved away from Thorvald to western Iceland where his wife's people lived. Following his family tradition, he committed manslaughter at least six times and was banished. He went only as far as a nearby island but, before he left Iceland, he had loaned a certain Thorgest the posts and boards of his sitting and sleeping platform. When Eric built his new home in exile, he demanded the return of the boards and was refused. He raided Thorgest's house and pursued and killed two of Thorgest's sons and some other men. He was exiled for three more years.''

"All that fuss over some boards?" interjected Frank.

"You have to realize that wood was scarce in Iceland. That was one of the reasons they traveled to North America. Having these boards was the difference between sleeping and sitting on the cold, hard earth or living in relative comfort," Marguerite explained.

"Go on," said Frank, becoming interested despite his objections.

"Not prepared to live on this island indefinitely, Eric sailed to Greenland around 982 A.D. By the way, he may have been the first travel agent. He named the country Greenland although it was notably lacking in greenery, because he was hoping to attract further settlers. When his exile ended, he returned to Iceland, unreformed, renewed his feud with Thorgest, was defeated, and voluntarily left again for Greenland. This time he traveled with thirty-five shiploads of prospective colonists, household effects, farm animals, horses, and dogs. Only fourteen ships reached Greenland, but, of these, all the settlers survived the first winter, in contrast with our Mayflower settlers, half of whom died that first year. Eric's children were Leif, Thorvald, Thorstein, and Freydis, an extramarital daughter.

"In the meantime, in 986 A.D., an Icelander named Bjarni Herjolfsson was sailing to Greenland and blown off course. Eventually, he sighted three unknown lands but did not go ashore. He turned around and sailed northeast back to Greenland. Judging from his sailing directions, the lands may have been Newfoundland, Nova Scotia, and Cape Cod. In his many travels to Norway and Greenland, he talked about these three lands.

"Leif thought these three lands should be explored and wanted his father, Eric, to lead the expedition, but, at the last minute, Eric backed out. Some people speculated at the time that Eric did not want discovery of a wooded land in a warmer climate to endanger his interests in Greenland.

"In 1003, Leif sailed without Eric and discovered Bjarni's three lands. This is not as difficult as it may seem to us, because the Vikings were proficient sailors and kept precise records of their trips with daily logs, much as ship captains do today. He sailed past the first land, presumably Newfoundland, went ashore on the second one, possibly Nova Scotia, and sailed two more days before he sighted land again, which, according to one theory, was Cape Cod.

"There are books full of information by the proponents of this theory, but I'll just give you a few of their arguments. For one thing, the ancient records state that they sailed into a sound between an island and a cape that extended north, and they steered to the west of the cape where they found a river that flowed down. They steered up the river and into a lake where they anchored and decided to remain for the winter, naming the place Vinland. A careful study of the writings and sailing directions has convinced many historians that they were on Cape Cod and sailed along the south shore, then up the Bass River to Follins Pond, which is very protected from the prevailing southwest winds and has underground springs for fresh water. There would have had to be a mooring hole to hold the stern of the ship. Frederick Pohl, who has spent years researching the Viking connection with Cape Cod, found several possible mooring holes in boulders in Follins Pond and other nearby areas. There are even two likely mooring holes in Sandwich at a formerly rich fishing ground, but those would have been from a later trip. Leif evidently stayed in the camp area for the winter and collected vines, grapes, and lumber. The grapes are important because they are not found in latitudes north of Massachusetts, unless we conclude that the climate was radically different then. Leif returned to Greenland and never sailed back to Vinland.''

"End of story, Marguerite. Those remains of Dr. Dafoe's were supposedly found in Eastham, not along the Bass

River.'' Frank had finished his sandwiches and was growing impatient. But Marguerite was not to be forestalled.

"The end of Leif's story but not of Viking explorations.
They were very interested in this warmer, fertile land. In
1005, his brother Thorvald sailed with thirty men to Vinland and explored the surrounding areas for three years.
They appear to have sailed south to Long Island and north
along the Maine coast. His were the first recorded meetings
with Native Americans; the Norsemen called them Skrael-
ings. In true Viking style, they killed the first group they
spotted, who happened to be sleeping. One survived to tell
about it and the Indians retaliated; Thorvald was killed by
an arrow and buried. His grave has never been located.

"In 1010, Thorfinn Karlsefni sailed to Vinland with sixty
men and five women. They stayed three years but left because of continuous warfare with the natives. Interestingly,
his son, Snorri, was born in Vinland and was probably the
first white American.

"Leif's half-sister, Freydis, was part of an expedition in
1014 and she evidently instigated and participated in a mass
slaying of some Icelanders with whom she and her husband
had disagreements. This is the first recorded crime in North
America.

"Frank, my point is that the Vikings were traveling to
North America for many years and were constantly exploring. Whether or not Cape Cod was Vinland is irrelevant
in this matter, because the Norsemen were exploring the
entire coast for many years. I have given you just a hint of
the available information. Peter Dafoe had access to vast
resources and may have been researching this in the university library and even the Boston library. He really might
have found a Viking skeleton. Remember the skull was
damaged. It may have been caused by a blow from one of
his own comrades, who then secretly buried him. This was
not unusual, as you can gather from what I have told you.

You know, Frank, I shall never again sit on West Dennis Beach without imagining a Viking ship sailing west past me and turning into the Bass River.''

''Marguerite, you must have been a wonderful teacher,'' said Medeiros grudgingly. ''You almost have me convinced. Especially if that skull turns out to be one thousand years old like the bone tested by Dr. Dafoe. We'll keep an open mind on this. But we are still considering other motives. Your nephew is not off the hook. He is still the only one known to be at the scene of the crime. Except you, of course.''

Chapter Eighteen

Joanne Parkinson, on duty at the dispatcher's desk, stared in unfeigned fascination at the trio of women and one man standing before her and demanding to see Chief Nadeau immediately.

The spokesperson identified herself as Mrs. Tyler Newcomb, her voice expressing the disdain for her surroundings that her words avoided. Although Mrs. Newcomb did not identify the other three members of the party, Joanne knew enough about the Dafoe case and the Newcomb connection to speculate as to who they were.

The elderly lady leaning on a cane with one hand and holding the arm of the gentleman with the other must be the redoubtable Rachel Stowe, aunt of Jebediah Newcomb. Even her clothes spoke of an earlier age. A black silk dress, its luster lost, bore at its neck an old-fashioned but magnificent lace collar, faintly yellowed with age. A silk fringed shawl, colors long faded, and held together with an elaborate jade pin, protected the frail shoulders from chill even on this warm day.

The gentleman on whose arm she leaned must be the lawyer, Joanne surmised, noting his briefcase, three-piece suit, and gold watch chain drawn across his vest. *He looks almost as old as she does,* mused Joanne.

The pretty young woman, trailing in the collectively grand wakes of her companions, is probably the wife.

Joanne was right on target. She was correct also in assuming that Portia's presence, lawyer though she was, was tolerated but not deemed essential.

Frank and Medeiros, surfeited by Marguerite's generous lunch and more than generous informational spate, were about to update their data chart in light of a plethora of new facts when the visitors were announced. Hurriedly turning the chart to face the wall, they braced themselves for the ensuing confrontation.

Jeb's mother, Mary Cinotti Newcomb, led the way and appropriated the centermost chair. Frank jumped up and offered the aged Rachel Newcomb his own comfortable armchair, but she declined, preferring a straight chair. The old lawyer and the young wife/lawyer fended for themselves.

As Albert Medeiros positioned himself to conduct this meeting, Frank hastily assessed the group, beginning with Jeb's mother, who had assumed leadership.

The private lives of public figures were public property, and Tyler Newcomb had provided good copy. Married first to the patrician beauty Anne Leland, he led the life expected of a Newcomb—exquisite little dinners in their luxurious apartment, charity balls, winter breaks in Palm Beach. Delicate since a childhood bout with rheumatic fever, Anne died of a collapsed heart valve at the age of twenty-seven. Freed by marriage from the importunities of his mother, now freed by death from marital circumscription, the thirty-year-old Tyler embraced the life of a man-about-town.

When, thirteen months after Anne's death, his father, Quincy, also died, pushing Tyler into the presidency of Newcomb & Stowe, ship chandlers, despite his being much younger than the minority partner, Silas Stowe, Jr., husband to his half-sister, Rachel, crisis loomed. The playboy was more at ease with maître d's than with ship masters.

At least until Mary Cinotti took him in hand. Newly hired as his secretary, the voluptuous Mary was a study in contrast to his late wife and to the young socialite women with whom he consoled himself. Dark and exotic looking as opposed to their pale prettiness, Mary would never be considered pretty, but she was beautiful in an exotic manner. Strong-featured with flawless symmetry, full-bodied with unexpectedly slim waist and legs, Mary chafed at the unfairness of her life. Denied access to higher education by an old-fashioned family structure in which the boys went to college and the girls went to secretarial school, she was determined to excel and surpass her favored brothers.

The opportunity came quickly when Tyler Newcomb began floundering in his new responsibilities. At only twenty years of age and less than two years with Newcomb & Stowe, Mary had assiduously applied herself to learning the business. Anticipating his gaffes, she subtly steered him to safety, but not so subtly as to escape his notice.

Eventually, he invited her out to dinner, more from gratitude than from personal interest. The gratitude lasted about five minutes, succumbing to personal interest, after he saw her for the first time garbed in an emerald-green dinner dress rather than her modest, tweedy office clothes. She was Mrs. Newcomb within a year and the de facto president of Newcomb & Stowe until the day Tyler died.

With Jeb now in Tyler's chair, her misgivings about his marriage were confirmed. Having breached the Brahmin barrier herself, and having never been accepted by them, she, nevertheless, had wanted Jeb to marry one of their daughters. Observing in Jeb the same irresoluteness in business matters as his father, she determined that he must marry someone who would cushion him financially. Failing that, he needed someone with business acumen to run the company without portfolio, as she had.

Portia failed her test on both counts. Orphaned and penniless, she brought no fortune into the marriage; intellectual but naïve in business matters, she would never be Jeb's Richelieu as Mary had been Tyler's. Portia's subordinate position in today's conference was synonymous with her position in the family.

Frank was shocked from his reverie by the reedy but imperious tones of Rachel Stowe speaking. Seated and no longer dependent upon her faithless legs, she assumed a new authority. Ignoring Medeiros, she addressed Frank, an employee of her town.

"Chief Nadeau, I must protest the shameful manner in which you have treated a member of the Newcomb family. My nephew, Jebediah, has had his name maligned by the gutter press solely because he had the misfortune to know this Dr. Dafoe, who managed to get himself murdered. We insist that you immediately issue a statement that Jebediah was in no way involved with this deplorable matter and that he, as the good citizen he is, was merely assisting the police with their clumsy and ineffectual investigation." Miss Rachel was never unintentionally rude.

"All of that and more, Mr. Nadeau," added Mary Newcomb. "His name is never again to be mentioned in connection with this case after you apologize, or this police department and your pokey little town will be sued from here to kingdom come. Particularly since you violated his constitutional rights and questioned him without his lawyer present. Nothing he has said has any standing in court. And you may be sure he will not speak with you again without legal representation."

"If I may," ventured Isaiah Hopkins, the last Hopkins in the firm of Hopkins, Rogers, and McNamara, "I think we can present our position in an amicable yet forthright manner. Mr. Newcomb has been harmed professionally, possibly irrevocably, by your misguided allegations. Perhaps . . ." and on and on and on. Isaiah was not of the new breed of attorneys for whom billable hours were the sine qua non. He was from a more leisurely era when gentlemen discussed differences at great length and decisions were reached without haste, if at all. He was obviously not a criminal attorney who would have cut right to the quick, thought Medeiros, but looked as if he had spent his entire career handling the business affairs of elderly women like Rachel Stowe and had an office crammed with musty papers tied in dusty ribbons.

Isaiah finally paused, his ancient lungs exhausted of air, and the two officers looked expectantly at Portia. They were not disappointed.

"I assume, since he was not arrested, that you brought no charges against my husband," she stated succinctly.

"That is correct, ma'am," answered Frank, relieved to hear a concise, nonthreatening statement.

"In that case, I would like to know the status of your allegations concerning him."

Medeiros caught the ball. "We have made no allegations regarding your husband and, as you concluded, there have been no charges brought. We questioned him and, you may be sure, advised him twice of his right to an attorney, which he declined and which we recorded on tape." The latter comment was directed to Mary Newcomb. "If you have some objection to his name appearing in the newspapers, you will have to take that up with the press. Neither Chief Nadeau nor I released any information about whom we were questioning. But people don't walk in here wearing hoods and, if they are recognized, the reporters have the right to identify them—freedom of the press, we call it."

Marguerite was irritable. She felt so restricted in the house, but her favorite summer retreat, a lounge chair on the patio, was denied her because of the milling group of reporters and curiosity seekers still attracted to the scene. Forced to remain indoors, she turned on her bedroom air conditioner and willed herself to ignore the distracting whine. Rusty positioned herself directly in front of the air flow and settled comfortably on the floor.

This mystery appeared hopelessly enigmatic. Jeb had admitted meeting Peter Dafoe, quarreling with him, and leaving him unconscious. But Jeb did not kill him, absolutely not! Yet the police claimed Peter was killed right on the spot, in her shed. There was only one explanation: Someone was following either Jeb or Peter Dafoe. Which one?

Since Jeb did not know the reason for the meeting with Peter Dafoe and had not had any previous contact with him or told anyone about their impending meeting, someone following Jeb would have been doing so for personal reasons relating only to Jeb—a jealous husband, an outsmarted business competitor (unlikely!), or some old vendetta. However, this murder appeared to be directly linked to Peter Dafoe and that terrible skull, because his cottage was searched, the green notebook taken, the library books mysteriously returned. Furthermore, Jeb was unharmed.

No, it was not Jeb who was followed, it was Peter. Running that through her mind, she visualized a possible scenario. A car followed Peter from The Landing. When he pulled into the school yard, the car did not enter because it would be seen. The school yard would not be an opportune place to accost Peter, because there were usually one or two other cars parked there in the summer. The murderer would not know if the cars were occupied or if the passengers were nearby.

Better to pass the school yard, drive a short distance, and reverse the car's direction. A car coming from the opposite direction would not be noticed, particularly by someone anticipating a meeting of great importance. The driver would hang back until Peter left his car and walked down the lane, then would follow, not too closely. A short way down the lane, Peter would have turned left and walked into the woods toward the shed. The murderer would have wanted to follow him into the woods, but could not because the lane was narrow and permitted the passage of only one car. He would not leave his car blocking the lane, not with murder in mind. What to do? Continue driving down the lane hoping for a place to pull over. And finding one! Egads, that was it! The pull off!

Over the years, the few residents of the lane had been meeting one another in cars heading in opposite directions and, tired of backing to the nearest driveway, had begun using a small area, free of trees and relatively free of brush, to pull to the side for one car to pass. The area had gradually become flattened, and its purpose would have been apparent, even to a stranger. Since the pull off was considerably past her property, and not on the route Peter had taken up the lane and through the woods, it might not have been searched by the police. She would search it!

How would she elude the crowd camped outside? Peering through the windows, she noted that the gawkers were all on the main road and not on the lane. Probably had the same problem as the murderer, she thought. No parking.

Exchanging her shorts for long pants and putting Rusty on a leash, she exited the house via the basement door not visible from the road, hurried down the steps, and gleefully slipped under the yellow police tape. *I have been wanting to do that,* she thought.

Walking down the path as quickly as Rusty's sniffing would allow her, she soon reached the infamous well shed and the end of the cleared path. Now it was into the woods where she would emerge onto the lane, hopefully out of sight of curious eyes. Rusty needed some tugging to force her through the dense areas, but, in quick order, they were on the lane beside her property.

She let the dog take her time now and they strolled ca-

sually down the lane, away from the direction of her home,
Rusty sniffing and Marguerite searching. In this fashion,
they came to the pull off, where Marguerite released Rusty
from her leash.

Not knowing what she hoped to find, Marguerite did the
obvious and looked for tire marks. There were many. This
pull off was used several times a day in summer, and the
murder had occurred three days ago. No help there.

Next, she searched the shrubs. No one walked into this
area. The few pedestrians tended to stay in the center of
the lane and did not detour into the pull off. Picking up a
piece of a fallen branch, she began to push the undergrowth
aside and poke through the accumulated leaves and
branches. Then she saw it! Clinging to the base of a shrub
on the shady, thus dark, side of the pull off was something
white. Using the stick, she freed it and discovered a handkerchief with some dark stains, not unlike bloodstains. And
clear as day was an initial—D. Dafoe or Della Robbia?

Dell's shoes were getting sand on the carpet in Frank's
office. For this he apologized, but not for his chagrin at
being summoned here.

He repeated the story of his activities on Friday night
without change. It was no big deal that the bartender at
Roy's did not remember him. He was only there about an
hour or so and the bar was busy.

Rosemary existed, despite the bartender not knowing her.
Same reason. He would go there this coming Friday and
maybe she would be there to verify his story.

Cynthia didn't see him? Well, he didn't see her either.
It was easy to miss someone if you were at different bars
on a crowded night. Particularly if you were only there for
an hour.

The job in California? It's there if he wants it. Pop assured him so and was anxious for him to take it. Hoped to

get him interested in fish instead of bones. Don't pay too much attention to Mr. Santangelo's account. He feels scorned.

The stained handkerchief? This brought a frown to Dell's face. "I don't know if it is mine. I do have some monogrammed handkerchiefs. My mother buys them for me. But white handkerchiefs all look alike to me, so I cannot identify it. That initial could be Peter's, you know. His mother is like mine. Always trying to spruce up their sons." Dell smiled at the thought of the preppy shirts and sweaters Julia frequently sent him. "By the way, is that blood on it?"

"We don't know yet, but this will be sent immediately to the lab for testing. And, of course, we intend to compare it with your handkerchiefs. Do you have one with you?" asked Medeiros.

"Sure," said Dell, pulling from his pocket a red print bandanna. "This is the kind I prefer."

A feeling of languor gripped Marguerite. Her excitement at finding the handkerchief and thus evidence of a third car and of someone following Peter had been quenched by Medeiros. If the murderer's car had parked at that site, it might have been Jeb's car. There was no evidence that he had parked in the school yard as he claimed. The handkerchief might have been Peter Dafoe's, taken by the murderer from Dafoe's pocket when he was searching for the missing bedroom key. It had probably been used to wipe fingerprints from the baseball bat. Of course, they were grateful to her and would pursue this lead but, at the moment, nothing changed with respect to Jeb Newcomb.

The continuous roller coaster of her emotions led to an unaccustomed indolence of mind and body. Tired also of the incessant phone calls from family, friends, acquaintances, and reporters, she had unplugged all the phones and was in isolation, trapped indoors, unable to tend to her beloved garden. She lay down on the sofa and forced herself, once again, to review this conundrum.

The chart at headquarters had several changes made on it, muddling the case further with each alteration.

Dr. Branowski had no viable alibi for Friday night or Saturday morning. His wife had been at their country home in western Connecticut for several weeks and he usually joined her there on weekends, but last weekend he claimed the pressure of work prevented him from doing so. Arriving home at six o'clock, he had remained home all evening, working, had no visitors, and no phone calls. A check on the neighbors to each side of him revealed that both houses had been devoid of occupants at the crucial hours. One family had gone to Maine for the weekend, and the inhabitants of the other house, two professors, had been out for the evening, returning after midnight. Dr. Branowski's garage door had been closed, as usual, and there was no way for them to know if his car had been in it.

The garage attendant in Back Bay knew Jason and his car well. The attendant was an aspiring actor and frequently consulted with Jason about auditions. He always kept a special eye on his car too, that neat convertible. He distinctly remembered that Jason had taken the car out at some time around seven o'clock on Friday evening and had not returned it by the time he had gone off duty at midnight. He was sure it was Friday night, because that was the last night he had worked before today, having been off on Saturday and Sunday.

The jitney rattled and bumped its way to the beach, a refreshing breeze wafting through its open sides. Only half full at this late-afternoon hour, Marguerite had room to relax and enjoy her release from the prison her house had become. All too quickly, the shuttle arrived at Coast Guard Beach and Marguerite clambered down the high step.

Instead of heading toward the water with the other beachgoers, she strode down the sand toward the dig. Familiar with their names from the newspaper accounts, she decided it was time to observe the team for herself. Her face unknown to them, she was able to mingle unnoticed among the other watchers, mostly in bathing suits, who came and went after short intervals of looking and failing to see dramatic discoveries. Archaeology is a methodical and often tedious science that, to an onlooker, appears routine and boring. It is definitely not a spectator sport.

Marguerite had very little interest in the how of it right now. She concentrated on the who of it. Dividing the team into two trios was fairly simple. It was easy to see who was giving directions and who was receiving them. The black girl, the Oriental young man, and the other obviously younger man were the three students.

Not interested in them, Marguerite focused on the three who had shared the cottage with Peter Dafoe. Cynthia Williams, a thin, blonde girl in chino cutoffs, a King's College T-shirt, and work shoes, looked intent and strained. She turned once or twice to the observers, but otherwise she fixedly avoided looking in their direction.

The two young men were a contrast in attitudes. The one with the glasses and old gym shorts looked irritable and occasionally groused at whichever of the students was nearest him. *That must be George O'Malley,* thought Marguerite, watching him closely for a while. He certainly has something bothering him, she concluded.

It was the other young man who claimed most of her attention, however: Anthony Della Robbia. Clad as usual in short shorts and tank top, he showed no resentment of the onlookers and even favored them with a smile or two. His sweat-slick face revealed no emotion, but his infrequent comments to his colleagues were even tempered, lacking the nervous intensity of his comrades' remarks. *Is this evidence of a clear conscience or of no conscience at all?* wondered Marguerite, thinking of the monogrammed handkerchief.

After almost an hour's observation, she began to discern order in the arrangement of the dig. Her attention was particularly drawn to an assortment of marker pegs, some of which appeared to delineate the proposed extent of the dig, and others of a different color that apparently indicated areas in which work had been completed. One of the pegs in the completed area was stuck in the ground wrong side up. No one paid any heed to it, except Marguerite. Could this be the place? She had to know.

A shiver ran through her. She at first attributed it to her thoughts, but, looking up, she realized the weather was changing. The sun was shrouded. Fog claimed the shoreline and the beach; enfolded the men, women, and babies, their blankets and umbrellas; then eased across the road, lapping against the buildings on its way.

A disorderly beach exodus was in progress, with the last of the bathers hurriedly gathering up wet, sandy blankets and cranky, sun-wearied children to trudge to the shuttle kiosk. Marguerite, unencumbered by such paraphernalia, walked briskly across the sand and up the path, arriving in good time to secure a place near the head of the line. She needed to get home and rest. There were important deeds to be done tonight.

Chapter Nineteen

Coast Guard Beach was more accessible at night than in the day during the summer. The small parking lot was open to visitors only after six P.M. Daytime beach users parked in a lot a mile away and queued for the shuttle bus.

Marguerite parked, slipped the car key into her shirt pocket, and grasped her Maglite. From the trunk of the car, she retrieved a small folding Army shovel, bought years ago for emergency use on ice or sand and cached in the trunk, waiting but never summoned.

With equipment firmly in hand, she walked across the paved area, past the showers, and down the boardwalk to the sand. Turning left, she continued along the beach, parallel to the water, until she reached the dig, at night resembling a moonscape, pockmarked and lifeless.

Aware of a gradual darkening, she peered at the black mystery above and noted the heavy cloud cover encroaching on the luminescence. The late-afternoon fog had dissipated, blown east by the southwest wind, but intermittent clouds persisted. She had hoped to avoid using her flashlight, but that hope now dashed, she turned on the light, partially shielding it, and searched the dig with a jaundiced yellow beam. It was an easy matter to locate the upside-down marker.

With great trepidation, she inched over the dig, careful to avoid stepping in a hole, and stopped at the suspect marker. Removing it, she uncovered her shovel, snapped it open, and began to dig. The soft sand offered minimal resistance, but its lack of cohesion caused it to slide down from the sides. With each small shovelful she removed, half a shovelful of neighboring grains fell back into the hole. In this fashion, she eventually dug a hole about one foot deep when she stopped to catch her breath and reevaluate her theory.

Perhaps she was wrong and was simply trespassing on an archaeological excavation. Lacking an alternate theory to exonerate Jeb, however, she willed herself to be right and decided to widen the hole before going any deeper. Digging on the side away from her, she soon struck something. Resigned to the probability of a rock or piece of driftwood but hoping against it, she knelt down and thrust her hand into the sand to reach the object.

It was not a rock or wood. It was softer and slippery, like plastic. It was plastic! Finally freeing it, her hand emerged with a tightly tied plastic bag. Ripping it open, she found another plastic bag and another. After the third plastic bag was torn away, she held in her hand a green spiral notebook.

Wildly excited, she reached again into the hole to ascertain whether anything else was hidden. Her search was interrupted by a car turning from the road into the beach entrance. She extinguished her light and ducked down flat to avoid the headlights, horrified to note that the car was not continuing up the road to the parking lot but was pulling into the no-parking beach dropoff area, perilously near the dig. Someone was coming here!

Without pausing to fill the hole, she grabbed notebook, flashlight, shovel; keeping low, she ran back up the beach. Now she blessed the dark night, so unwelcome just a short time ago. More than a hundred yards up the beach, she spied a grass-covered hummock. Ducking behind it for cover, she peered back toward the dig and, as the moon cleared, saw a faint shadow moving in that area. It must be the murderer, checking the notebook's hiding place. With a gaping hole in its stead and the sand that was removed still wet, the conclusion would be obvious. She had to get away.

From this point on the beach and extending for about a hundred yards, small cliffs, formed by incessant erosion, overhung the sand. Hugging the cliffs to lessen her chance of being seen, Marguerite reached the boardwalk. She would have to exchange the relative shelter of the cliffs for exposure on the circuitous walk. Looking nervously behind her, spotting no one but too blind in the dark to be sure and afraid to linger, she made a dash for the walk and ascended it speedily. Retracing her earlier steps, she passed the showers and continued up to the parking lot.

Never had a car looked so welcoming. She ran to it, opened the unlocked door, hurled everything onto the passenger seat, and jumped behind the wheel. Simultaneously locking the door and reaching into her shirt pocket for the ignition key, she froze. The key was gone! She never lost keys. Checking her pants pockets and rechecking the shirt pocket removed all doubts. The key was gone. It must have fallen out when she knelt and reached down into the hole.

Feeling dangerously vulnerable trapped in the confines of her car in a nearly deserted parking lot, she quickly debated her next move. Locked doors and windows were flimsy barriers. If she could return to the main road she would be safer, but to do so meant passing the murderer's car. She had convinced herself that it was the murderer who had parked there. He might have decided to wait there, ready to follow her car rather than chase her across the beach. Her fear did not permit her to choose that route.

The only hope was to use her superior knowledge of the area and escape on foot by an alternate route. Blocked from access to the road, she would use the path to the visitor's center, familiar to her from her many walks and bicycle rides along it, but possibly unknown to her pursuer.

Eschewing the bicycle entrance to the path as being too far down the parking lot from her present position, she opted for the cover of the woods at the upper pedestrian entrance. Its beginning was treacherous on this dark night, a series of steps, the number unknown to her. Afraid to use her light, she bent down to feel each step as she descended, her difficulty compounded by the cumbersome shovel and Maglite, carried for the purposes of defense and illumination, respectively, and by the precious notebook. Tucking the notebook into her waistband, she tightened her belt to secure it.

Safely down the steps, her path continued downhill with single steps interspersed along the way. In dread of falling but terrified of pursuit, she pushed herself faster than normal caution would have allowed. Noting the bridge ahead in a momentary clearing of the moon, she stopped and listened carefully. This was the spot where the bicycle path joined the walking path. A pursuer from below the area of her parked car who had spotted her entering the pedestrian path could have entered the bicycle path intending to intercept her here—if he was familiar with the geography.

Pausing for a few moments and hearing no untoward noises, she started forward, then hesitated, waiting for the clouds to obscure the moon. The short respite allowed her to catch her breath, and she went rapidly across the bridge, feeling unduly exposed.

Back onto the pavement and keeping to the edge close to the cover of the trees, she continued at a moderate pace, too apprehensive to use her flashlight and equally apprehensive of falling. Her heart was pounding, her breathing labored, but adrenaline fueled the engine. Several times she heard cracklings of twigs or the ping of loosened stones and stopped to listen, but she reached no conclusion. The woods were full of nocturnal animals whose movements sounded very much like a human pursuer. Just keep going!

About a mile into her escape, she came to an intersection of the Salt Pond walking trail and the bicycle path, and plunged into the narrow dirt walking path, judging that a pursuer would miss it and continue down the wider bicycle path. As soon as she was safely out of sight of the bicycle path, she paused to listen for any footsteps coming down the pavement. Hearing none, she felt a smidge safer and, with renewed confidence, groped her way through the wooded path.

Close to the end of the walking path, she had one more dangerous spot where it again intersected the bicycle path. Wanting to avoid that path and a possible pursuer, she decided to swing left onto the Button Bush Trail for the blind. The moon was totally obscured and she could not distinguish her route. Forced to choose between blundering in the wrong direction and using her light, she briefly shone her light and located the rope that guided one along the Button Bush Trail. Relieved to be nearing the end of the trail, she began to plan her next move. Going home was too dangerous. Better to walk straight out to Route 6 and then to police headquarters to be rid of the notebook that was making her a target. She would stay at a motel tonight—luckily her wallet was still in her pocket—and by tomorrow the murderer would know she no longer had the notebook and would lose interest in her. She hoped!

Of course, Rusty had to be walked tonight. Perhaps she could prevail on that nice Officer Morgan to walk her. Satisfied that her problems were resolved, she was startled to hear running footsteps behind her. Distracted by her planning, she lost her attention and reacted too slowly. Raising the protective shovel, she began to turn toward her pursuer when she was hit hard on the side of the head and fell over dazed.

Slipping in and out of consciousness, she was vaguely aware of shouting and commotion around her. In one of her moments of lucidity, she felt raptorial fingers trying to free the notebook from the tightly cinched waistband where she had secured it. Opening her eyes and seeing the grim visage of Anthony Della Robbia leaning over her, she screamed.

Chapter Twenty

Awakening this time to full consciousness, Marguerite saw Jeb hovering solicitously about her.

"How can I ever thank you, Aunt Marge?"

"You can start by not calling me Aunt Marge," she groused, putting both hands to her head in an attempt to quell the jackhammers within. "Where am I?"

"In the Cape Cod Hospital, Aunt Marge . . . er, Aunt Marguerite."

"Have I been here long?"

"Since about midnight. It's eight A.M. now. You had quite a blow on the head."

"I remember now. That beast of a murderer hit me and stole the notebook. Did he get away? Who found me?"

"Did who get away?" asked Jeb, confused.

"The murderer! That Della Robbia fellow."

"Aunt Mar . . . guerite, he was not the murderer. He saved your life. Cynthia was the murderer. She hit you over the head and was about to hit you again when Dell tackled her."

Marguerite closed her eyes again and let her head sink back into the pillow. This was too much to absorb with her head pounding as it was. Perhaps if she just rested for a minute . . .

At nine she was awakened by the nurse checking her vital signs. Still on concussion watch, she was not permitted to sleep too long. The sanitized sterility of the hospital room and the nurse's pristine garb were too much for Marguerite's still-aching head.

"Please close the blinds," she moaned.

"Now, now, Mrs. Smith. You want everything to look nice for your visitor, don't you?" answered the nurse.

"What visitor?"

"The police chief of Eastham, Frank Nadeau."

"Good," said Marguerite. "Maybe I can make some sense of this now," she added, struggling to sit up.

"Stay just as you are," commanded Nurse Martin. "I shall send an aide right in to straighten your bed and help you freshen up."

Deciding it was too painful to resist, Marguerite allowed herself to be cosseted by the amiable aide. Refreshed but not relieved of her headache, she awaited Frank, who tiptoed in, looking as if he had need of the aide's ministrations. Sleepy-eyed, unshaven, rumpled, he nevertheless summoned a big smile for her.

"*Bonjour,* Marguerite. *J'espere vous êtes bien.*"

"*Tant bien que mal.* Now please tell me what happened. Jeb told me Cynthia was the murderer."

"Yes, she was. Luckily for you, we had confirmed all the other alibis by last night and had narrowed it down to either Jeb or someone in the cottage."

"That sounds like everyone. Who did you eliminate?"

"Jennifer's boyfriend, for one. When we discovered that Jason had taken his car out of the garage on Friday night, Medeiros arranged for him to be questioned in Boston without Jennifer present. He became frightened and admitted his true whereabouts Friday night. We were right in suspecting that his expensive life-style was not supported by acting, or by waiting tables, either. He had given up the job at Julio's and was a paid escort employed by a top-of-the-line service. With his looks, clothes, and savoir-faire, he was in great demand. Managed to get tips and presents on the side too. Jennifer did not know about this other life of his, and he was terrified she would find out. He doesn't want to lose that pot of gold, either. That's why he stepped forward so quickly to give her an alibi—it protected him also. We checked with the escort agency and he was engaged on Friday night from about nine-thirty P.M. to three A.M. When he left Jennifer at about nine-fifteen that night, he claimed he was going to meet his theatrical agent.

"That cleared him, and we didn't think Jennifer would have done it alone. Besides, that parking ticket on her car was legitimate. She was in her apartment alone from nine-fifteen and was grateful to Jason for the alibi he supplied."

"Which other suspects did you clear?"

"Dr. Branowski, the head of the department. His alibi is even more delicate, and I am not at liberty to discuss it. But he was accounted for."

Marguerite wrinkled her forehead, guessing at the secret, and immediately regretted it, as even that movement exacerbated her pain.

"And you still suspected Jeb, didn't you?" she scolded.

"Yes, but he was only one of the suspects. The three people in the cottage were also suspects because of professional reasons. Finding Viking remains would have made any one of them instantly famous. That is quite a temptation.

"Cynthia and George appeared to alibi each other, because George was awakened at ten-thirty P.M. by the noise of Cynthia trying to open the bathroom door. That left Dell, and he had no real alibi. Cynthia had not seen him at Roy's, the bartender did not remember him or the mysterious Rosemary as being there that night, and that handkerchief was his. We went to the cottage with him and he had two others just like it. He claimed that anyone in the cottage could have used it, but we decided to watch him."

"Why did he follow me?"

"He didn't. He was following Cynthia. Dell has good analytical powers. He knew he was a prime suspect and wanted to clear himself. After we identified the handkerchief as his—by the way, that was blood on it—he knew the murderer was someone in the cottage. Since both Cynthia and Dell were claiming to have been at Roy's but did not see each other, and since he knew he really was there, he suspected her. Especially since he went out onto the dance floor a couple of times and was sure she would have seen him if she had been there. So he decided that she had the notebook hidden somewhere and would retrieve it. We thought he had the missing notebook and, after all the heat we had put on him, he might move it to a safer place. Officer Morgan was assigned to follow him. When Cynthia went to the dig, Dell followed her, and Morgan followed Dell. You know the rest. Cynthia struck you, Dell tackled her, and Morgan ran up and handcuffed her."

"But it was Dell I saw reaching for the notebook," she protested.

"Yes. You were hurt and he knew you would be taken to the hospital. He didn't want the notebook to be lost. He handed it over to Morgan for safekeeping."

"Why did Cynthia wait so long to attack me? I was almost at the end of the trail when she struck me."

"She had not expected to find you at the dig and had no weapon. The shovels were in the other cottage and she had no excuse to ask for one, so she would have used her hands to dig in the sand for the notebook. Remember, she only weighs about a hundred pounds. She could not take on someone like you, no offense intended, one-to-one, particularly since you had that big flashlight as a weapon. Maybe she saw the shovel too. It was only when you turned on the light near the end that you illuminated a fallen branch she could use as a club. It was long enough to keep her out of your reach. As soon as she was able to pick it up, she ran for you. She was about to hit you again when Dell tackled her.''

"I guess I owe that young man a thank you.''

"It's worth at least a glass of iced tea," he teased.

"Frank, try to be serious." She sniffed. "You still have not told me why she killed Peter Dafoe.''

"Jealousy and greed. It seems she loved Peter. Had since the first time they met. Thought he wasted himself on Jennifer. Cynthia could not stop talking after we arrested her. There's so much pent-up bitterness in that girl. Bitterness about Peter, about Jennifer, about Branowski, about Dell. She believes everyone conspired against her, even you.''

Marguerite shivered a little as Frank continued.

"Peter ignored Cynthia as a person; she was just another would-be archaeologist. Friday night, when she saw him at The Landing, she wanted to talk with him but had to get rid of George. She took him home and headed right back to The Landing. Peter was outside in the parking lot on the telephone and she heard him talking to his mother and leaving the message for Jennifer. That's how she learned he had made some kind of a discovery, but she did not know what it was. She suggested to him that they become partners. He had a flair for discovery and she was superorganized. She could be of great help in planning, recording, cataloging, and writing the resultant papers and books. They would be a team.

"Peter seemed to be weighing her suggestion, but she overstepped herself and indicated they should be a pair. She would be an asset to him; Jennifer was a drag.

"Peter became furious at this slur about his wife and began calling her names. Said he would never be interested in a woman like Cynthia. He had a real woman. Cynthia cried when she told us this part of the story and could not bring herself to repeat everything he said.

"She tried to calm him down with an offer to be just his professional associate, but he accused her of using him because she would never be more than third-rate. With that he left.

"She knew he was meeting someone and would probably reveal his secret; she followed him, parking exactly where you suggested the murderer had parked. After hearing what he told Jeb, she realized the magnitude of his find and that it was the chance of a lifetime for her. Still smarting from his insults, she hated him now and wanted to erase the memory of his taunts. When Jeb left she went into the shed, saw the baseball bat, and hit him with it several times, releasing her fury. Then she took the bedroom key from his pocket, went outside, wiped the baseball bat of fingerprints, and threw it aside.

"She had seen Rusty run into the woods with the skull and tried to find it, but someone came onto the deck of the house nearest the shed and turned on the light. She had to end her search. That was when she decided to lock the shed door, hoping the body would not be found until she had a chance to come back and locate the skull."

"The body would not have been discovered if Jeb had not been coming with the boys. I only went down there for the clamming gear," Marguerite volunteered.

"So Jeb helped us to solve this, after all," said Frank.

"Yes, he did. But go on."

"Cynthia went back to her car and noticed some blood on her hands, sneakers, and the lower part of her pants legs. She wiped her hands and sneakers with Dell's handkerchief, which she had borrowed, as he surmised, threw it away, and rolled up the legs of her chinos. She didn't get home until after eleven, but, as she told Peter, she is a superb planner. George was sleeping soundly—she heard him snoring—and she knew Dell was not home because his car was missing. She slipped quietly into the living room, changed into her pajamas, and hid the clothes under the sofa. Then she changed the time on the kitchen clock, left the kitchen light on, went into the bathroom pulling the door hard enough to stick, and made a lot of noise trying to open it. George woke up and helped her open the door. She steered George into the kitchen, noting that it was now about ten thirty-five P.M. He returned to bed.

"She pretended to do likewise and, as soon as she heard him snoring again, went into the kitchen and corrected the time on the clock. None too soon either, because Dell came home shortly after."

"But didn't you say she was at Roy's?" asked Marguerite.

"That's where she got lucky. She never went into The Landing when she returned there on Friday night, because Peter was in the parking lot. The next day, when she needed an alibi, she stuck with the story she had told George when she drove him home and said she went to Roy's figuring it would be crowded and no one would be expected to remember her. By a stroke of fate, when Officer Morgan showed her picture to the bartender, he identified her as being there on Friday night. This threw us off the track and made us think Dell was the one who was lying. It seems that Cynthia had been there on Thursday night and the bartender did speak with her. In the busy season, one night blends into another and, when Morgan asked about Friday night, he thought that must have been the night."

"That was a one-in-a-million piece of luck for her," said Marguerite.

"Yes, and a piece of bad luck for Dell, who really was there. But it was not only Cynthia's phony alibi that made him suspicious. You see, Dell is something of a lady's man and he notices women, even the ones he is not interested in.

"Saturday morning, when Cynthia left for the dig at the

same time as they did, she delayed pulling away from the cottage until they drove away and she then went back into the cottage, leaving the motor running, unlocked Peter's door, and took the green notebook and the library books about the Vikings so no one would know he had been researching that subject before she made the big discovery. In her haste, she closed the bedroom door but neglected to lock it. Then she took her clothes that had been hidden under the sofa bed and examined them. The sneakers had to go, the T-shirt was okay, and the pants were only stained on the bottom. Accustomed to frugal living, she cut the legs off the pants and turned them into cutoff shorts. She dropped the books in the library box and threw the sneakers and pants legs into the woods behind the library and hurried to the dig, having excused her lateness by claiming to need something from the drugstore. She wanted to search for the letter Peter had told Jeb he received from a lab about the carbon dating, but did not have time because she had seen Violet Barlow going down the walk toward a cottage and had to be gone before she returned. She hoped to find another time to search the bedroom.

"When, on Monday, she suddenly appeared in chino cutoffs that she had not had before, Dell remembered that she had shown Sergeant Patterson a pair of long chinos and claimed to have worn them Friday night. Dell knew that she had two pairs of long chinos because she shared the closet in the bedroom. He looked in the closet Monday afternoon and saw only one pair of long chinos, checked her laundry bag without finding the other pair, then noted that her sneakers were not in the closet. She had three pairs of shoes: sneakers, sandals, and work shoes. The sandals were in the closet and she was wearing the work shoes.

"Knowing by then about his handkerchief, which was at the scene of the crime, he assumed she might have borrowed it as she sometimes did borrow things. That is when he decided to follow her,'' Frank concluded.

"Lucky for me,'' said Marguerite.

"Yes, it was, but you might not be so lucky another time. You had better keep out of police business hereafter.''

"I would have stayed out this time if I had known you suspected someone other than Jeb.''

"Trust us. We can't announce everything we know when we are working on a case.''

"Hmmph! There is still something I do not understand. Why did Cynthia bury that notebook in such a public place? It might have been dug up by anyone.''

"It was only supposed to be there for a few hours, and she had to get rid of it quickly. There was no safe place in the cottage, because even if Peter's body had not been found, he might have been reported as missing and the police would be involved. She couldn't leave it in her car, either, because it would link her to the murder and she could not delay too long in getting to the dig on Saturday morning. She took some plastic shopping bags from the cottage, placed the book in them, and put the package in her knapsack, which she carried every day to the dig. Very risky, but she had no option. At noon, when the rest of the team halted for lunch and walked up to the shade of the shuttle kiosk to eat, she made an excuse about needing to complete something and said she would join them in a couple of minutes. As soon as they were gone, she dug a hole in one of the completed areas and waited for a moment free of onlookers to bury the notebook and replace the marker upside-down, intending to come back that night.

"However, the body was prematurely discovered and she was with the police most of the night. On Sunday, the police visited the cottage twice and she was afraid they might be watching her. When suspicion fell on Dell Monday, she thought she was clear and went to retrieve it.''

"That is all for now, Mrs. Smith. The doctor is here to see you," cheerily announced Nurse Beggs, bursting in, red-haired and freckled with a fresh young smile, a counterpoint to the bossy Nurse Martin.

If rest was what Marguerite needed, she got very little of it. Portia was her next visitor, overflowing with gratitude and bearing messages from Marguerite's children. Alexandra was on her way to Cape Cod. Thomas was standing by and would be there if her condition warranted. Marguerite assured Portia it did not.

Immediately after her light lunch, consommé and Jell-o, the room was brightened by Dell bearing a huge smile and an enormous bouquet of red roses interspersed with daisies (marguerites) and a two-pound box of Ghirardelli chocolates. The starving Marguerite attended first to the candy. After a couple of pieces comforted her, she turned to Dell, still partially concealed by the flowers, and said, "Well, young man, I guess I have to apologize. I thought you were the murderer."

"No apologies necessary, Mrs. Smith. You saved me from being charged with that murder."

"Nonsense! The police were following you. They would have seen Cynthia digging up the notebook."

"Yes, but she could have claimed that I buried it there and that she suspected so because of the upside-down marker. All the evidence still pointed to me. Even her alibi had been mistakenly confirmed. It was only because she followed you and attacked you viciously that her story came apart. I owe you everything, Mrs. Smith.

"I guess Frank Nadeau was wrong, then. It's a good thing I did interfere."

"It certainly is. By the way, now that we're friends, Mrs. Smith sounds so formal. Do you mind if I call you Aunt Marge?"

Epilogue

The three undergraduate students, reluctant archaeologists heretofore, had such an exciting summer that they returned to King's College full of enthusiasm, declaiming to all the wondrous thrills of fieldwork.

George O'Malley, with a new confidence in his ability to relate to fellow humans, completed his doctorate and returned to Hoboken, where, having been offered a position at a New Jersey college, he could now afford the elevated rents, a product of gentrification.

Cynthia remains in jail awaiting trial. As the most educated person there, she began teaching classes for incarcerated women.

Dell completed the summer's excavation with distinction and, in the fall, was awarded his Ph.D. and Peter Dafoe's position at the university with the likelihood of attaining tenure. His parents, desolate at first, came east for an extended visit and decided that Boston was tolerable, particularly after Julia discovered Newbury Street and Dominic discovered the North End, which was the perfect place for a seafood restaurant specializing in Pacific fish. He had been under pressure from Julia to find an appropriate place in the business for his soon to be son-in-law, Arthur, and would name him manager of the restaurant. Dominic and Julia took an apartment in Boston and visit several times a year.

211

Dr. Branowski quietly resigned from King's College. Liberal colleges overlook many peccadilloes on the part of staff, but the involvement of undergraduate students made this one impossible to ignore. He is selling antiques from his home in western Connecticut.

Jennifer Dafoe, now a wealthy woman in her own right, dispatched Jason. During the funeral preparations, she had reached rapprochement with Mrs. Dafoe. Bereft of her only child, Victoria Dafoe found in Jennifer her only link to Peter and quickly set about making Jennifer suitable for this honor. Aided by Mrs. Dafoe's tutelage and hairdresser and dressmaker, she became a society beauty—the Widow Dafoe, Jr.

Marguerite had no peace that summer—the media, family, and friends saw to that. It was with relief she opened her mail one day in August to discover a first-class round-trip ticket to San Francisco, courtesy of the Della Robbia family, and a reservation at the Mark Hopkins Hotel for two weeks. At least she would have six hours of peace on the plane.

Jeb and Portia's lives changed significantly. Rachel Stowe had been aware for some time of Jeb's business deficiencies and his disastrous real-estate ventures. She dreaded the possibility of the Newcomb homestead in Eastham being sold and the property subdivided for modern houses. It was their heritage and should be preserved for young John Quincy and James Denis. Consequently, she changed her will and designated the house as a museum dedicated to the great sailing captains of Cape Cod. All the furnishings and artifacts were to remain. She left a large trust fund for its maintenance and named Jebediah and his sister, Lucia, as joint salaried trustees. Belatedly, she recognized her previous neglect of Lucia, probably because her personality was so much like that of her mother. But, to her credit, Lucia has her mother's business aptitude too.

Lest Jeb be too crestfallen about his lost inheritance, Rachel bought back the stock Jeb had sold to his mother and sister and made provision in her will for him to inherit it. Advised by Aunt Rachel of these changes, Jeb accepted them gracefully and began spending longer and more productive hours at Newcomb & Stowe. He may actually have turned over a new leaf. Only time will tell. Isaiah Hopkins took Portia under his wing and convinced her to leave the high-powered firm for which she worked and join Hopkins et al. She did so and began to assist Isaiah in handling the old money and old estates, including the Newcombs and Dafoes.

As for the Vikings, who knows? Rachel Stowe decided to permit a modest excavation of her property under the guidance of that charming young Della Robbia fellow, whose first task was to decipher the green notebook that was written in a code devised by Dr. Dafoe. The Vikings might well have selected that beach for a camp, Miss Rachel concluded. It was chosen by the Newcombs, wasn't it?

If this book has whetted your interest in pre-Columbian voyagers to the shores of North America, you might want to read additional material. I suggest the following books:

Fell, Barry, *Bronze Age America*. Boston: Little Brown and Company, 1982.

Pohl, Frederick J., *The Lost Discovery*. New York: W.W. Norton & Company, Inc., 1952.

Severin, Tim, *The Brendan Voyage*. New York: McGraw-Hill Book Company, 1978.

—Marie Lee